DUST

CHRIS MILLER

Death's Head Press

Houston, Texas
www.DeathsHeadPress.com

Cover Art: Justin T. Coons

The "Splatter Western" logo designed
by K. Trap Jones

Book Layout: Lori Michelle
www.TheAuthorsAlley.com

BOOK 3

This book is for Aliana:

You gave me the title, and with it came the story. Thank you, babe. Now, dig those heels into the stirrups and hang on. The forecast is calling for rain and scattered body parts.

This book is also for Cerberus (Mike, Patrick, Me): World Domination.

PART I:

ON THE TRAIL

1

TEXAS, 1879

THE BLOOD DRIPPED and slinked down the wall behind the man with the gaping head wound. The others around the table merely sat there, slack-jawed, their cards locked in their hands, cigarettes and cigars smoldering in the corners of mouths and between fingers, thin tendrils of blue smoke snaking into the air of the saloon. On the table before them lay a pile of money, bills and coins, and there was even a rather fine pocket watch, its *tick-tick-ticking* becoming the only audible sound now as the ringing in their ears receded.

The watch belonged to the dead man with the giant hole in his head. You could see through it—the man's head, not his watch—if you didn't mind the stringy goo which slopped viscously through the hole, or the meaty gray pulp that slid slowly down the wall among the rivers of blood like macabre slugs.

There was movement behind them, the shuffling of feet, and a grunt. The man behind the bar was going for something. Then came the sound of a cocking hammer.

The man with the still-smoking gun produced a

second revolver in his left hand and aimed it at the man behind the bar without ever turning his gaze from the shocked men at the table with him.

"You're in the process of making a poor decision there, partner," the gunman said coldly. "I recommend you put that scatter gun back where you found it before I scatter your brains like Mr. Pocket Watch here."

He gestured to the dead man with his first revolver and finally turned his gaze to the man behind the bar. He could see the rest of the patrons of the saloon, all of them frozen in fear, clutching their drinks and women tightly to them. To a person, the expressions of their eyes were identical.

Saucers.

"What do you say, Hoss?" the gunman asked politely.

The barman, a large and hairy sort—three hundred pounds if he was one—took a few moments to glance about the room, gulping audibly before slowly nodding and returning the double-barrel shotgun to its spot beneath the bar.

"Excellent," the gunman said, turning back to the men at the table. "Say, you boys want another round? I could go for another myself. Been riding all day. A man gets thirsty, especially in this time of history."

Some of the eyes at the table narrowed slightly at this, but none said a word.

"Any takers?" the man asked, still holding his pair of six-shooters out. "Come on, it's on me. Hoss? Round us up some beers here for my pals and me."

No one moved. No one spoke. No one acknowledged they'd heard the gunman. He turned his gaze back to the barman.

"Go on, now," he said and gestured with his gun. "We're thirsty."

The spell over the barman seemed to break then and he began to shuffle awkwardly. He fumbled with some glasses under the bar—the chimes of glass clinking together and the still *tick-tick-ticking* of the dead man's watch were the only sounds—and began pouring the drinks. The room remained thusly silent until the barman finally came and placed a glass before the gunman. Foam slopped over the brim and dripped to the table where it pooled around the base of the glass. With a shuddering sigh, he then placed one in front of each of the others at the table. No beer spilled from any of these.

"That'll do just fine, Hoss," the gunman said, a pleasant smile on his face. "Now, you hustle on back to that bar and keep your customers happy."

The man did, a dull expression of fear on his face. The gunman returned his left-handed revolver to his hip, then picked up his beer. He looked around the table at the other men, none of whom had moved since Mr. Pocket Watch had been dispatched.

"What should we drink to, fellas?" he asked them as he raised his glass.

No one spoke.

"Come on now, we're just making acquaintance here, we gotta drink to something, right? I know, how about this?"

He leaned forward and rested his revolver on the table but did not remove his hand. He met each one's eyes in turn before he spoke.

"Information."

He raised the glass to them all and drank deeply

several gulps. A satisfied *'aahhh'* accompanied the clunk of glass on wood as he roughly sat his glass down. No one joined him.

"Boy, I can't wait to get back to when they serve this stuff cold. So much better, you just have no idea."

The others just stared, confused astonishment on their faces.

"Now," he went on, nodding toward the dead man, "Mr. Pocket Watch here, he had information I need. But he was holding out. You see, I've been here for quite a few years now, and I know I'm getting close. But I ain't there yet. That's why I need some information. And, truth be known, I think you boys know about as much as Mr. Pocket Watch here. Every one of you. So that means I really only need one of you to get what I need. Now, I don't see any reason for any more bloodshed here in Hoss's fine establishment. So, I'll ask you boys like I asked Mr. Watch: I'm looking for two things. A man who goes by the name of Dreary, and a little town called Dust."

He let the question hang in the air as he gazed around at the men. As he did, he took another long draw on his room temperature beer—and with the heat outside, room temperature was about eighty degrees, give or take—awaiting a response.

Finally, he got one.

The guy to his left, a small man wearing a pair of spectacles and a bowtie with his black vest, and sporting a pencil-thin mustache, gulped loudly, his throat clicking, and opened his mouth.

"Good sir," he began in a polite drawl, "this town you speak of, uh, Dust was it?"

The gunman nodded.

"Dust, yes, well," the man coughed. "I can tell you I've never heard of the place, and that's the honest truth. But this—"

The gunman's revolver rose from the table and aimed at the man's face. His hands went up instinctively and his eyes nearly crossed to look down the barrel.

"I better not catch the whiff of a lie come outta you, mister," the gunman said flatly. "I've got business with Dreary and Dust, and I mean to see to it."

The man nodded frantically, his throat clicking some more.

"Y-yes, I-I understand," he said, near panic. "I-I was just saying this Dreary fellow, I think I may know where you can find—"

"You watch your tongue, Leroy!" another man at the table said, the one sitting on the other side of the bowtie man named Leroy.

The gunman's gaze shifted to the other man. He wore a ten-gallon hat and had a thick and bushy mustache he might have called a handlebar mustache where he'd come from, but these men would know nothing of that term.

"I suggest you let Leroy talk, mister," the gunman said. "We're having ourselves a conversation here and you're interrupting. Interrupting gentlemen when they're conversing is rude. I don't appreciate rude behavior."

The man just glared at him for a long moment, then finally looked to the table, clutching his fists in frustration. The gunman returned his gaze to Leroy and nodded for him to go on. The man's throat clicked some more, and he continued.

"Dreary, uh, there was a man come through here a couple weeks back. He was looking for this same town you are, this Dust place. None of us heard of it before, but Roscoe here," he nodded in the direction of the rude man, "told him where he might find what he's looking for. An old lady by the name of—"

Roscoe move like lightning and there was an explosion of sound as Leroy's skull exploded out of his right temple, showering a meaty pulp of brain and bone in a viscous, hot bath of sticky blood across the gunman's face. A gasp flushed through the room like a rehearsed play, and Leroy's lifeless meat-husk was toppling out of the chair to the floor, eyes crossed and tongue lolling.

The gunman spat a wad of brain from his mouth as his revolver swung to Roscoe and a thunderous *boom* erupted from its barrel. Roscoe's throat tore apart, flesh and sinew and blood slinging about the men on the table, ropes of crimson arcing into the air.

The gunman thumbed the hammer on his revolver as Roscoe's gun went off. A woman screamed behind them as the gunman fired a second time, this one taking off the top of Roscoe's head as though it had been packed with TNT. Slushy pulps of gray and red erupted and spattered all about the room as more screams came.

The gunman was aware of the barman making for the scatter gun once more and, with a sigh, drew his second revolver. The barman's face seemed to burst as the round went through his cheek and exited his temple, every feature of the man's face coming off as though torn away by an invisible specter.

"Goddammit, Hoss, I warned ya!" the gunman

snarled, swiveling around with both guns on the other two men at the table with him.

They both stared, terror in their eyes, and looked from the barrels to each other, then back to the gunman.

"Now," the gunman said with a slight growl, "I hope we've weeded out all the rude folks here and can have a friendly fucking conversation. What do you say, boys?"

They nodded emphatically and told the gunman everything he wanted to know. His frustration gave way to a satisfied grin as they told him what they knew. When they were done, he stood, holstering his guns, and he nodded to the two men.

"Much obliged, gentlemen, much obliged. Could have been that easy from the start. Shame things had to go the way they did."

He leaned over and shoved the pile of money toward them, plucking the pocket watch from the pile and slipping it into his pocket.

"Something to remember you boys by," the gunman said with a smile. "Y'all feel free to split that amongst yourselves. I suppose I'll be on my way now. I got gods to kill."

The remaining two men and the rest of the saloon stared at him incredulously, utter confusion upon their faces.

"Just who in the hell are you, mister?" one of the men at the table said as the gunman's silhouette filled the entrance, the swinging saloon doors opened to either side of him like a pair of wings.

He turned to them with a smile they could barely see with sun at the man's back. He tipped his hat to them with a nod.

"Name's Mr. James Dee," he said. "And I ain't from around here. But you'll be damn glad I came before long."

Their confusion remained as he turned and stalked into the onset of dusk, his spurs chiming as he vanished from sight.

2

JAMES DEE RODE nearly a week in a southeasterly direction before coming to the place the men at the saloon had told him about. The place where the woman resided. The trail was hard, but he'd seen worse. He'd been through far worse terrains in places a universe away. At least here the terrain was recognizable. He knew it, understood it. Perhaps it wasn't *exactly* the way he remembered it—and God-willing he would be able to see it that way again—but it felt closer to home than he'd been in a very long time.

He was a large man, solidly built and taller than most. His broad shoulders nestled into his long coat as the sweat moistened and cooled his back. Beneath him, his steed made a sound as it blew through its lips, and he eased back the reins, slowing them to an easy walk. No need to run or gallop anymore. They were here. The place Dreary had been heading and the place where he would find the old woman who had the answers he needed.

The gunman and his steed eased out of the piney woods to the dirt road leading into town. The trees thinned as they neared, and a sign made of planks of old wood stood before them as they crossed into the township.

Winnsborough.

A faint grin spread across his face as he read the sign and the dusty clops of his steed's hooves carried them steadily into town. It wasn't long before he found the tavern—the only one in this dirt-speck of a town—and he looped the reins about the post outside and headed in through the batwing doors.

The place was largely deserted, being that it was midday and most folks would be working their fields and shops about town. Still, there were a few patrons. A man whose hair shined with oil played a happy tune on the piano at the far end of the establishment and a pair of old-timers sat at the bar, their considerable bellies holding it up as they nursed piss-yellow ales. The bartender, a thin man in a bowtie and a clean-shaven face who couldn't have been more than twenty-five years old, wiped the inside of a glass with a towel. A woman in a fluffy dress that revealed the majority of her gargantuan bosom—and did little to hide the rest of her bulbous figure—leaned next to the old timers, presumably doing her best to peddle her pussy.

All but the piano player looked up at him as he entered.

He stood there in the frame of the entry, a hand on either swinging door, holding them open. He took them all in, gazing into their eyes in turn until each looked away. The piano continued its jingle, the player seemingly lost in his ditty.

James stepped into the establishment and let the doors swing loosely behind him, flapping like the wings of a bat until they lazily settled into a crooked recollection of closed. He made his way to the bar, deliberately staying down near the end away from the old-timers and the whore. They all looked up at him again warily as his boots *clonked* on the planks, his spurs jingling quietly. He tipped his hat to them and nodded. They did not return the gesture. The old-timers turned back to their ales, the lady back to her prospects.

The barkeep continued wiping down glasses, occasionally glancing up at James for a half-second at a time before turning back to the task at hand. The glasses nearly sparkled, and James knew the young man was simply avoiding his gaze.

Finally, James rapped twice on the bar and said, "Barkeep."

The young man froze in his efforts, the towel deep in another glass, but he did not meet his gaze.

James frowned and rapped once more.

"Barkeep, a word if you will."

A moment passed before the young man finally tossed the towel down and placed the glass with the others. He then wiped his hands on his apron and shuffled slowly down to the end of the bar toward James. As he neared, he put his hands on the bar as though to steady himself, and finally looked him in the eye.

"What can I get you, mister?" he asked, an annoyed but also wary tone in his voice.

"Well," James said, tipping his hat high on his forehead, "maybe you can get me a few things. Let's start with a shot of whiskey and a glass of whatever that piss-water is the gentlemen down there are nursing."

A hint of a glare seemed to enter the young man's face for just an instant, then it was gone. He went to work pouring the drinks and returned, setting them down roughly in front of James. The beer sloshed and some foam spilled over the lip of the glass. James smiled at this, but only to himself.

Barmen.

"That'll be a nickel, lest you wanna start a tab," the barkeep said, the same annoyance and waver in his tone.

James stared at him hard, a thin smile on his lips as he dug out a coin and flipped it to the bar where it bounced and flipped noisily for a moment before the young man reached out and slapped his hand down over it with a loud clap. His face was red, the forehead encroaching on purple.

James's hand shot out and clamped over the younger man's wrist like an iron restraint. The barkeep's face continued to redden, but the annoyed look started to border on shock as his eyes went wide.

"Do I know you?" James asked as he leaned in close. The barkeep struggled to get his hand free, to absolutely no avail. He didn't answer.

"I asked you a question, boy," James said as he pulled the kid's arm across the bar. "Mighty rude to ignore a man when he asks a direct question, wouldn't you say?"

The young bartender's face was all alarm now as he struggled in futile attempts to free himself of James's grip. "I-I never seen you before in my life, mister!" he said as he pulled with his arm. It went nowhere.

"That's exactly what I was thinking too," James

said. "I's thinking to myself, 'I ain't never seen this boy in my life, yet he's acting like I come in here and shit on his breakfast.' Seeing as I did *not* come in here and shit on your breakfast, what do you say you cut the tough guy act with the stranger in town and act like a goddamned gentleman, sound like a deal?"

The younger man quit struggling, his face flushing of color, and he sighed. After another moment, he nodded a few times.

"Excellent," James said and released his arm. The man immediately began massaging his wrist.

"Will there b-be anything else, mister?" he asked, averting his eyes.

"As a matter of fact, there will," James said as he threw back the shot of whiskey and took a long draw on the beer. He was pretty sure it *was* piss. "I'm looking for some information, and in all my dealings it seems the best place to find information is the local tavern. If the barkeep don't know, usually one of the patrons do. Seeing as your patronage is pretty thin right now, I figured I'd just start with you."

The bartender just stared at him, confusion and a hint of angry fear painting his face as the color returned.

"Let's start with something easy," James said. "What's your name, boy?"

The barkeep's face darkened at the insult, obviously not fond of being referred to as 'boy'. Still, he held his tongue and only answered the question.

"My name's Marcus."

"Marcus!" James said and slapped the bar with a laugh. "That's good, that's good. Well, Marcus, I'm Mr. James Dee. I ain't from around here. Well, that's not exactly true, but it ain't exactly a lie, neither. But that's a long story. We'll save that one for another time. I'm looking for someone. A couple of someones, actually, but we'll start with the lady."

Marcus continued to stare at him warily.

"Lady's name is Miss Agatha Dupree. I hear tell she's from Winnsborough, though I can't rightly say just *where* in Winnsborough. I have urgent business with her, and she'll want to see me. Do you know Miss Dupree?"

Marcus's eyes narrowed to slits as he finished massaging his wrist and let it fall to his side.

"What kind of business?" he asked suspiciously. "You looking to hurt little old ladies?"

James laughed out loud and took another gulp of the piss. He smacked a sigh that wasn't quite satisfaction as he replaced the mug on the bar.

"Marcus, my boy," James said, still laughing and wiping foam from his lips. "Do I strike you as the type of man who goes around hurting little old gray hairs? Honestly, I'm offended!"

James put on a phony wounded look for a moment before resuming his laughter.

"I just ain't in the business of giving out folk's whereabouts to strangers, is all. Forgive me, mister, but I don't know you from Adam and we ain't exactly got off on the best foot here."

James's laughter died all at once and his face grew hard.

"I believe that was due to your rude behavior to a weary stranger coming in off the trail merely looking to quench his thirst."

Marcus looked down at the bar again and sighed, embarrassed.

"Now," James said, softening his face and his tone, "if you'll be so kind, where can I find Miss Dupree? Rest assured I mean her no harm at all."

Looks from the old-timers and the whore down the bar drew Marcus's attention for a moment, but he eventually looked back to James and nodded.

"Alright," he said. "You head east out of town. 'Bout a quarter of a mile past the town limits you'll see a cottage on your left, has a big ol' shed to the side of it. Big Oak out front. They's a rope swing hanging from it, but she ain't had kids in the house in ages. That's her place. But if she asks, I'll tell her I ain't said nothing, you hear me?"

Marcus was pointing at James now. James nodded reassuringly.

"Your name won't pass my lips, Marcus, I can assure you."

Marcus seemed satisfied with this and nodded, lowering his finger. He started to move back down the bar when James stopped him.

"There's still the matter of the other someone I'm looking for."

Marcus froze, then turned back to him.

"A man," James went on when he had Marcus's attention again. "Goes by the name of Dreary. *Gear* Dreary. Not sure if that's his given name or not, but it's all you hear on the trail. Gentleman type, tends to wear a bowtie and one of those bowler's hats. Big beard and—"

"You don't want nothing to do with him, mister," Marcus said, cutting James off.

James looked perplexed. "Now why would you say such a thing?"

"Marcus is right," the whore at the end of the bar said, stepping around the two old-timers. "Son of a bitch come in here, oh, I'd say a week ago now. Looking for that same lady you is."

"Is that right?" James said, turning to face her, leaning against the bar with his beer in hand. "What business did he have with Miss Dupree?"

"Far as any of us know, same as you," she said as she perched herself a couple feet from him on the bar. "Wouldn't say. Said they had business to discuss. Man gave me the willies, though, I can tell you that. Looked all up and down me while he's in here, then I offer to let him have a poke and he turns me down! Can you believe that?"

James laughed as he finished his beer and set the glass on the bar.

"Ma'am, I cannot imagine what would possess a man to turn down a poke with such a *fine* specimen as you."

He smiled broadly as she rolled her eyes and blushed.

"Oh, don't be an asshole," she said. "I know I ain't the cat's meow, but this bitch can make you purr. When you close your eyes, a wet snatch is a wet snatch. Most men, that's all they care about. But not this fella, Dreary. You know what he said to me?"

James shook his head. "No, ma'am, I sure do not."

She leaned in close and he could smell sour beer on her breath under a far too thick musk of perfume and sex.

"He says, 'Madam, your offer—while appreciated—is tantamount to an investment in molten lava. It will surely melt one's genitalia to a smooth stump, but then its fire will soon be snuffed and all one is left with is useless stone'. Can you believe that shit?"

James was stifling a laugh. "That's a new one on me, miss."

He turned, threw another nickel at Marcus, who caught it in midair. He then tipped his hat to the patrons, even the pianist still chiming away in the back.

"I appreciate the information and conversation, folks. I best be on my way."

He turned to leave and felt a hand on his arm. He turned to see the whore, pulling gently on his forearm. She was pressing her breasts together with her arms to the point they nearly toppled out of the dress and the brown of her nipples showed plainly.

"What's the rush, honey?" she asked, fluttering her eyelids at him. "Got time for me to make your day?"

James smiled widely and put his hand over hers as he leaned in close to her face. She began to turn her face up to his, as though he were going to kiss her.

Then he stopped, only an inch from her face.

"Madam, I prefer to dip my wick in clean wax."

He pulled her hand off his arm, turned, and walked out without another word. As the batwing doors swung in and out and he mounted his steed, he could hear her yelling from within the tavern.

"You teasing son of a bitch!"

He whistled to his horse as he tipped his hat once more to the tavern's entrance and rode east out of town.

3

HE FOUND AGATHA Dupree's cottage just where the barkeep had said it would be. It stood off the trail a fair distance, plumes of smoke billowing from its chimney, the flaking white paint on the siding adding a charming layer of patina to the home. A large covered porch sat welcomingly in the front of the place, and a network of iron ore stones traced a path through the dooryard to a post where James tied the reins to keep his steed in place.

An old woman sat on a wooden rocking chair on the porch, gliding to and fro lazily as the old thing creaked over the slats of the porch. James smiled charmingly at her as he traversed the iron ore path to the front, tipping his hat to her as he approached. Her face was set, but not hard, a curious expression etching her features. Beside her sat a glass with a what could have been lemonade or irony water from the well out back. He didn't know which.

"Ma'am," he said as he came to the stoop and rested one foot on the first step. "Lovely afternoon we're having."

The woman's lazy rocking never ceased as her

eyes—and *only* her eyes—scanned him over appraisingly.

"*I'm* having a fine afternoon," she said in the unhurried drawl of East Texas, an accent James found nostalgic. "But I don't know who the hell *we* are."

The rocking persisted and silence fell between them. It was not an uncomfortable silence, but neither was it a comfortable one. James cleared his throat.

"Ma'am, I must beg your pardon, I've forgotten my manners, I—"

"Have to've had some to've forgotten them," the woman answered curtly, one eyebrow raising ever so slightly.

"I'm, uh, sorry, ma'am," James went on, struggling to find the right words. "Been quite some time since I've had use for them, I'm afraid. But I do have some, I assure you."

The woman's head joined her eyes as she made a second scan of him from head to foot and back again, resting on his eyes. Hers narrowed.

"Why do you look familiar?" she asked, a note of pondering in her voice, as though she were trying to resurrect an ancient memory.

James smiled. "I can't rightly answer that ma'am, but let me start over here. My name is Mr. James Dee. I, uh . . . well, I'd say I ain't from around here, but that's not rightly true. Not entirely. But you see, there's a man I'm looking for. But not just a man, you see, I'm looking for a town, as well. One I've been searching for these past seven years since I arrived in this place. I hear you might be—"

"You're looking for Dust and the gentleman outlaw Gear Dreary," she said, matter of factly as though this were settled science.

James was taken aback and his chin retracted. He had been told this woman was knowledgeable, but he hadn't expected this. He didn't know just *what* he had expected, but this wasn't it.

"Why, yes ma'am, as a matter of fact, I am. How did you . . . ?"

"A man searching for a single town for seven years and not finding it is either an imbecile with a compass or he's looking for Dust. No two ways about it. And a man looking for Dust on the heels of another man is looking for Gear Dreary."

James was astonished, and his hanging jaw proclaimed his awe.

"He come through here a few days ago," she went on, ignoring his surprise. "Same as you, looking for Dust. Mighty dandy fella, I'll give him that, but it don't hide what I can tell in a man right off. You see, I been blessed by God or maybe cursed by the Devil—haven't decided which it is just yet—with the ability to know things about people just by laying eyes on them. And I've also been blessed—or cursed—with knowing how a body can find themselves in Dust, though there's few who seek it with honorable intentions. Nothing there but evil, and I prefer it to stay there. If it were to get out, God help us all."

James leaned forward, his elbow propped on his knee, reeling in his jaw. He was fascinated by this mysterious woman, and he simply couldn't contain his awe.

"Ma'am, that is mighty inciteful," he said, allowing

the awe to transcend his voice. "How'd a lady such as yourself come to be here in Winnsborough?"

She made a dismissive wave with her hand.

"You ain't here to write my biography, boy, you're looking for an outlaw and a terrible place. Don't go chasing rabbits that don't got a damn thing to do with what matters."

James's jaw clicked shut audibly and he did the thing with his chin once more as he felt his cheeks flush.

She stopped rocking then and leaned forward in her chair, her hands on her knees. Her eyes, a brilliant blue he noticed for the first time, grew hard and bored into him. He could feel them digging beneath his flesh and he suddenly felt as though he were naked before her. His flush threatened to turn purple, but she leaned back and nodded once, then smiled for the first time. It wasn't broad, but it was kind. Almost familiar.

"You ain't like him," she said.

James didn't know what she was talking about for a moment, then it came to him.

"Like Mr. Dreary, you mean?"

"I do," she said with a nod. "He come through here a few days ago, as I said. Looking for Dust just as you are. But I could see in that man something dark and fierce. That evil residing in Dust, he wants to harness it and use it for himself. But you, well . . . you seem to have a different purpose."

James just locked with her gaze and said nothing.

"You were right when you said you ain't from around here, but it's more than that. A conundrum. It's both the truth and lie, all at once. You *are* from around here, but you ain't from around *now*."

James's color vanished. It was as though the woman had looked directly into his brain—into his *soul*—and seen all his secrets laid bare. *That* was why he'd felt so naked before her. He *had* been naked before her.

This woman is something else, he thought.

"I knew you looked familiar," she said as she stood from her rocking chair. "I'll tell ya where to find Dust, mister, but not Mr. Dreary. Fact is, I can't rightly say where he is. But it ain't Dust."

"Have we met before, ma'am?"

A thin, bullet-fast smile passed over her face and vanished.

"No, but we will. We have."

James's eyes narrowed for several moments, curious as to her meaning. This woman was full of mystery, but now was not the time to explore how they'd met. Or when.

"You didn't send him that way, I take it? Dust, I mean?" James said, prompting the woman on and dismissing his curiosity.

"Christ on His throne, *no!*" she proclaimed, a hand covering her heart. "The very *last* thing this world needs is a man as black-hearted as Dreary finding Dust and harnessing what lurks there. I'm not sure you yourself are ready for what you might find, but there's great power in you, mister. I can see that. You've seen many a thing in your travels, but what awaits you in Dust is something you've not encountered before."

"I have to get there, ma'am," James said, placing his foot back on the ground and rising to his full height. "I've an understanding of what awaits me there, if limited. But no matter the cost, I have to find it and stop it. The future of mankind rests upon it."

She regarded him for a long moment, her head cocking to the side ever so slightly as she did.

She nodded. "Yes, I suppose it does. You have a pure heart, Mr. James Dee. You were even a good man once, before your travels changed you."

An almost silent bark of laughter escaped him and he put his hands to his hips before he realized he'd done it. He quickly dropped them to his sides again.

"Ma'am, I—"

"Oh, don't try and bullshit me, son," she said, swatting the air. "You have a pure heart, but you're not a good man. Not anymore. Maybe you will be again, but until your journeys are over, you can't be. Good men aren't capable of doing what your mission requires of you, but the pure heart . . . well, that's necessary. And by the Christian God and all the lessers, I dare say you have one."

James took a step back and returned his hands to his hips. She was right. In all his years and travels through the unknown, the goodness had been stripped from him. *Torn* from him was actually a better assessment. It had been required so that he could do what had to be done. A good person wouldn't shoot a man in cold blood to get the information he needed to go after the horrors of the universe. Only a hard and cold man would do that.

Yes, the woman was right.

"If I've offended you, I apologize," she said. "You may live yet to redeem your soul, but you need to be hard for now. For the storm that's coming. Dust is closed off for now, but it won't last forever. The

Others told me when I was still a girl one such as yourself would be coming along. One such as Dreary, too. I never figured it would take so goddamn long for y'all to arrive, but here you are. I sent Dreary on a goose hunt. But he'll be back. *You,* on the other hand, need to get to Dust and do what needs doing before he returns and finds his way there. Do you understand me, Mr. James?"

He looked up at her beneath the brim of his hat and nodded coldly.

"Good," she said. "Now listen up. I'm only going to say this once, and it's closer to rocket science than you may think."

It took James a moment to realize what she'd said. He wasn't confused by the terms—he'd heard them before—but he couldn't believe the woman had used it. Not here.

Not *now*.

His face must have betrayed his shock because she smiled.

"You ain't the only who's not from around . . . *now*."

James laughed and shook his head.

"Lady, I'm listening."

4

GEAR DREARY PULLED the telescopic lens from his eye and collapsed it down to the size of a large thimble before slipping it into the pocket of his vest. He struck a match and hovered it over his pipe for a moment and began puffing plumes of smoke. He waved the match to put it out, dropped it to the grass, and smashed it beneath his heel to be sure the embers were out.

"Man's headin' out, Gear," a burly man next to him announced, looking through his own collapsible telescopic lens. "Headin' east."

"Indeed he is, Quentin," Dreary said, a charming southern drawl on his tongue which hinted at education and etiquette. "I am presently observing such myself."

Quentin glanced back at him from his perch by a pine tree, confusion riddling his face.

"W-wha—"

"Never mind, Quentin," Gear said as he pushed off his own pine which was across the trail and in the woods a spell from the lying old woman's cottage. "We've business to attend to. You and Avery head on after our friend heading east, but don't be seen. We want him to arrive at his destination. He's going to lead us there, you see."

Quentin nodded as Avery, a wiry man in stained trousers and tunic, stepped to the horses behind them, and Quentin joined him.

"Mr. Bonham," Dreary said as he turned to his left, away from the other two, "you and I must visit the lady here. She's caused me considerable frustration and cost me dear time. I do believe there's some recompense due."

Bonham was a tall man, broad shouldered, a thick mustache perched upon his lip and week-old stubble littering the rest of his features. He smiled, though no teeth were visible behind the whiskered forest of his face.

They mounted their horses and headed toward the cottage as Quentin and Avery set out after the man heading east. Dreary knew the man. Well, didn't *know* him, per se, but knew *of* him. The man who seemed to appear out of nowhere years ago in the town of Duncan, north of here on the Chisolm Trail, and who'd been hunting the same place Dreary had for years. And they were so close now. He could feel it. Could almost taste it. But the elderly hag had tricked him and sent him off into Indian territory, and they'd damn near been killed for it. One of his men, Charles, had paid the ultimate price for the misdirection, and Dreary meant to see justice for the infraction.

Their horses clopped lazily out of the trees and onto the trail, and they made their way up into the dooryard of the old woman's cottage. She was sitting in her chair, rocking lazily as she had been before the exchange with Dee, and seemed none too surprised to see them approaching.

"I thought you might be back," she said as they dismounted their horses and strode up onto her porch. "Must say I thought there'd be a little more time."

There was no fear in her voice or on her face. Only a quiet dignity and resignation.

"I do apologize for disappointing you so," Dreary said as he tipped his bowler hat to her. "We had the misfortune to cross paths with a tribe of savages which halted our progress. My man Charles was killed in the skirmish. They took his scalp."

"Is that all?" she asked, an amused look in her eyes as her brows rose. "A shame they didn't take his balls."

Dreary laughed then, but his eyes remained cold.

"They did indeed, madam. They took his scalp after."

The old woman reeled back then, howling laughter and slapping her knee with a furor he might not have thought possible in the frail old woman. But she wasn't really frail, he knew. She only appeared to be.

"Well," she said between guffaws, "I reckon that was worth it, then!"

More howls of laughter ensued, and Bonham looked to Dreary, his hand on a blade in his belt. Dreary halted him with a hand.

"If you're quite finished," he stated. It wasn't a question.

The old woman laughed a few more times, wiping tears from her eyes, and finally settled down.

"Just get on with it, Dreary. You're not getting anything from me, and we both know it."

He smiled and nodded. "I do not delude myself so as to believe otherwise, madam. But you see, I don't need anything from you. Our mutual friend, Mr. James Dee, has all the information I need to find Dust, and he's being trailed as we speak. Mr. Bonham and I shall join them directly."

Her eyes grew cold and hard and she stood then, glaring at Dreary with an intensity which almost made him flinch.

"Unfortunately for you," she said, her teeth grinding together and bared, "you have no idea who you're dealing with in Mr. James Dee. I thank the good Lord and all the lessers I'll get to watch him burn you and yours to the ground like a hay fire in July."

She spat on him then, a thick, slimy thing, and it stuck to his considerable beard. He closed his eyes, shielding most of his frustration and disgust, and fetched a handkerchief from his breast pocket. He wiped his face clean, folded the handkerchief, and replaced it.

"Madam," he said, the slightest waver in his voice as he locked his cold, gray eyes with hers, "I do abhor violence. I find it revolting and undignified. But what I find even *more* revolting and undignified is a liar. You *lied* to me about the location of Dust. We'd have been happy to leave you be. All we wanted was to arrive at that elusive town of myth. But you lied to us. It doesn't matter now, what's done is done, but I'm a man of justice. I cannot let such a crime go unpunished and I can*not* abide a liar."

He turned his head to Bonham and issued a brief

and shallow nod. There was a metallic *schlink* as the blade was drawn from Bonham's belt and the big man moved forward as Dreary took a step back.

"There's nothing worse than a liar, madam!" he said as Bonham drove the blade deep into her solar plexus. She gasped, spitting blood. "Hell was built on the lies of the Serpent!"

Bonham ripped the blade down with jarring speed and strength, and stepped away from her as her intestines spilled from her opened abdomen like noodles from a bowl. She spat black blood from her mouth as her lips moved, though no words came out. She collapsed to her knees and Bonham slipped behind her as Dreary looked down past his nose at her, one corner of his lips turned up in a cold smile.

She spoke a final time.

"Like a hay fire in July," she croaked through pints of blood.

"We shall see, madam," Dreary said as he tipped his hat to her once more and nodded to Bonham behind her. "Farewell, my dear Miss Dupree."

Bonham dragged the edge of his blade across her throat, high-pressured jets of blood spraying her porch and chair as he did, digging in past and through her windpipe. There were gargled screams which carried no volume, and before he was done sawing, they had stopped altogether.

As Dreary mounted his horse, the old woman's severed head was dropped in the dooryard, mouth agape and coated in gore, her brilliant blue eyes filming over. Bonham mounted his own horse, then wiped his blade on his trousers before returning it to his belt.

"There's a lesson to be learned here, Mr. Bonham," Dreary said as they turned to the trail and began to pick up speed to catch up to the others.

"Oh?" Bonham replied, little more than a grunt.

Dreary smiled and nodded.

"Never poke a serpent," he said. "They're vindictive buggers."

Bonham made a half smile as they rode toward Dust.

5

JAMES NEARED THE landmark Miss Dupree had described to him just before nightfall. On one side of the trail stood a mighty oak, its massive limbs sprawling majestically in all directions, its leaves golden and sparse. About four feet from the base, just where all the major limbs split into their various networks of wooded arms, stood a goat's skull, seeming to glare directly across the trail. It was much too large, James deduced, to be that of any normal goat. Its horns were thick and coiled, and the remaining teeth were menacing and sharp. It was nearly two feet across at its widest, he guessed, and he began to wonder if it were fake. He decided it didn't matter in the end; this was where the woman had told him he would find the trail to Dust.

"Just across from the giant goat head, you turn into the woods," she had told him. "Try to keep your angle just so, no more than forty-six degrees, no less than forty-three. If you hit it just right, you'll find the trail. Otherwise . . . you'll never see it at all."

Some odd magic, he supposed, or perhaps it was ingenious engineering on behalf of the town's founders. Dust didn't *want* to be found. The old woman had made that clear. The ones from the void had made that clear to James himself many years ago when he'd learned of all the abominable gods and had begun his crusade. Though this place hadn't been where he'd started. He'd begun in another place—another *world*—entirely, one wholly alien to him. The next five had been equally foreign. This was the closest he'd come to being back home, though he was still roughly a century from his birth. He often pondered—since his seven-year journey from Duncan to Winnsborough had begun—if he were not to succeed on this current mission, he was unsure if he'd see his birth at all. If he were to fail, would he simply fade into nothingness? Would he blink out as though he'd never been?

Would it matter either way?

It would not, he concluded. And if he were to fade away or blink out or whatever happened when the past reset the future, he could not stomach the possibilities that failure would hold for the likes of the one person in all the countless universes he still loved with all of his ever darkening heart. The one person he envisioned when his resolve wavered. The one who would not be if he failed to be.

Joanna.

But he could not dwell on her now. It had been nearly two decades since he had seen her, yet her face was still ever present in his mind. He found it difficult to push her image aside for the task at hand, but he would have to if he were to focus and get the job done. Dreary would likely be hot on his trail before long, the old woman had warned him of this, as well. And while he meant to see Dreary in the ground should they ever cross paths, Dust was of far greater import.

He veered off the road at what he guessed to be between forty-three and forty-six degrees. He kept his steed steady and moving, first into the brush, then between the pines and oaks and dogwoods, the road vanishing behind them. He would not travel all the way into Dust in the dark, but he would find the trail and then make camp. Tomorrow, Dust awaited, and his mission therein.

He moved between the trees, maintaining his angle and returning to it every time he was forced to veer off around a tree or bramble. He counted in his head as his steed clopped along over the dead pine needles and crunching leaves.

"Ninety-seven paces of your horse," Miss Dupree had said. "Then you turn perpendicular to the road you just left. If you do it right, you'll be in the middle of the trail to Dust. If not, you'll have to begin again."

Ninety-one . . . ninety-two . . . ninety-three . . .

He trudged on, his focus absolute, nothing else existing in all the world for him in that moment. He could feel the still warm air of early autumn swirl around him as a faint breeze wandered its way through the trees. The sweat cooled on his neck and his brow, then dried to a tacky finish on his weathered skin before being replaced by fresh droplets. He wiped them away.

Ninety-six . . . ninety-seven.

"Whoa," he told his steed and pulled at the reins. The horse stopped at once, and obeyed as James tugged to the right. A moment later, he looked up and a narrow trail lay before him. It hadn't been there a second before, he was sure of it. But this did not cause him to marvel any more than finding a dog shitting in the street might. After all the places he'd been and all the things he'd seen, this was a relatively unremarkable event.

A sign, little more than a plank of wood with poorly painted letters on it hung to the right of the trail, nailed into the pine it hung from, sap droppings smattering its top and running down in dried streaks.

DUST, it proclaimed, and was accompanied by an arrow pointing eastward. James Dee smiled broadly, slipping his '72 Winchester repeater from the holster on his steed's saddle and cradling it across his lap.

"Found you, you son of a bitch," he muttered to himself as he clicked with his mouth and nudged the horse into motion.

He headed deeper into the woods toward the mythical, damned town.

PART II:

COMPLICATIONS

6

DENARIUS KING SPRINTED through the woods, his frantic breathing bursting from his lips in loud, excited hitches. His eyes were wide and desperate, and he glanced back over his shoulder every twenty paces or so to see if they were still following him.

They were.

"You're a dead nigger!" he heard one of them call to him through the trees as he ran, the *clump-a-dah-clump-a-dah-clump-a-dah* of their horses' hoof-falls an ever-increasing drumbeat in his ears.

He darted around an oak and nearly sprawled as he tumbled through the golden-green branches of a dogwood, his arms spiraling to knock them away from his face as though they were spider-webs. His heart was racing. His lungs were burning. His mind was reeling. Where could he go? What could he do? He had only the bloody knife he'd taken from the stupid one, Josephus Tarly; the one he'd buried to the hilt in the idiot man's throat not ten minutes earlier when he'd made his attempt at escape.

He was a free man, had been a free man more than a decade now. President Lincoln had seen to that. Three-fifths of a man, but a *free* three-fifths of a man. But these men seemed to disregard the decrees of Congress, instead opting to take him and treat him as property. He'd barely managed to keep his wife and child hidden from them when they'd come, Wild Bob, Taggart, and Josephus. He prayed they were safe. That they were *still* safe.

I'll get back to you, Marlena! he thought frantically as he dodged around another oak and several pines. *You and Martin stay safe!*

Then his foot caught on a loose patch of leaves and his legs were no longer beneath him. He hit the forest floor hard with a loud *oomph,* the wind rushing from his lungs. Constellations of black stars danced in his vision for a moment as he gasped for air, trying to struggle to his feet again and falling once more.

Clomp-a-dah-clomp-a-dah-clomp-a-dah.

They were close. Very close. He had no time to lay sprawled on the ground. They were nearly on top of him, but he could hardly breathe. His yellowed teeth bared as he grimaced, desperately trying to suck in air and regain his footing. He had to move if he were to—

Something struck the back of his head just as he regained his stature and he was back on the ground, face down. He didn't remember the trip. There had been a knock to the back of his head, then he was on the ground. The interim journey had been skipped entirely.

Denarius was faintly aware of Wild Bob climbing down from his horse about ten feet in front of him, though his main focus was on getting his world to stop swirling like the undercurrent of the ocean during a hurricane. He rolled to his back, wincing in pain and gasping for breath. His hands instinctively went to the back of his head to nurse the knot forming there.

"Goddamnit, you think you can kill one of my boys and just take off?" Wild Bob shouted as Taggart dismounted. "You got a reckoning coming, boy!"

Denarius spit dirt and pine needles from his mouth and managed to get up on his elbows, scooting away from the approaching men, desperation on his face.

"Please, suh," he said, putting one hand before him in either surrender or to ward them off. He didn't know which. "I gots a family. I ain't done y'all no harm. I just want to get back to my wife and boy's all. Why y'all doing this?"

The whining note in his pleas caused his stomach to twist, but he was unable to wrangle it into a more dignified tone. His lips quivered and he could feel the sting of tears in his eyes.

"I ain't meant nobody no harm, never!" he nearly shouted, though the whine was still present. "And I's a free man now! Making my own way, just like y'all! Let me be to see after me and mine, that's all I want!"

Wild Bob and Taggart glanced at each other in turn, then began laughing hysterically, their mostly toothless mouths jerking open and shut beneath their unkempt beards, ropes of spittle slinging from them like glistening cords in the twilight. As they laughed, they drew their revolvers.

"I don't give a good goddamn what Congress says you are!" Wild Bob said as his laughter died down to a chuckle. "Congress is a thousand miles from here. 'Round these parts, your black ass is worth a purse of shiny coins. Well, the right parts of you is, anyhow."

Terror streaked Denarius's features, etching deep lines of horrified angst around his eyes and mouth. The dimples in his cheeks that Marlena found so handsome now looked like pits of pitch in a charred landscape of fear.

"Please, suh!" Denarius pleaded, on his buttocks now and both hands before him. He *was* in a posture of surrender now as he made his way to his knees before the approaching men. "What's wrong with you folks? What I done to y'all? Ain't you got no souls? Ain't you God-fearin' men?"

"God-fearin'?" Taggart asked, speaking for the first time. "The only one doin' any fearin' 'round ought to be you! God ain't got shit to do with your kind. Nothing but a knuckle-dragging ape with a goddamn voice box. All you're good for is working fields and filling our purses. And that big black cock of yours will bring a fine payday for Wild Bob and me."

Taggart drew a large knife with his free hand.

"Now drop trou and let's make a eunuch of ya!"

Denarius screamed as they descended on him, but his scream was cut short when Taggart's face burst out in a meaty pulp, leaving behind a dripping red skull, one eye glaring wide and lidless, jaw hanging open. The ringing in Denarius's ears blocked whatever Wild Bob was saying—or *screaming,* from the looks of it—as he turned and dropped to the ground, his revolver up and at the ready.

Taggart's body finally collapsed to its knees, the one lidless eye still glaring in what Denarius thought was fury, confusion, and a certain sense of awe. Then he collapsed forward with a meaty thump to the forest floor before him, face down, and never moved again.

The ringing was beginning to wane, and Denarius could hear Wild Bob's words now. Frantic, panicked barks.

"The fuck's happening?" he screamed. "Who the fuck's out there? You done killed a good man, god-damn you! I'll see you hang for this, you hidin' son of a bitch! Come out and show yourself, you coward!"

Wild Bob's eyes were as wild as his name. They darted this way and that, and Denarius realized the man wasn't paying him any mind at all. He remembered the bloody knife he'd dropped when he'd fallen, and glanced around for it. It was to his left, the crimson stain glistening on the blade, and he snatched it up.

"The law's on *my* side 'round here!" Wild Bob was crowing into the forest, which was thickening with shadows that seemed to move and crawl with the gentle breeze. "You hear me? The law's on my—"

Denarius buried the blade deep into the man's calf. Wild Bob had just come cautiously up on his knees, his revolver before him, pointing in all directions in turn. Denarius was sure he'd seen a tear leaking from the corner of one of the man's eyes.

After the hilt of the blade butted against the soft flesh of the man's calf muscle and the screaming began, he was sure both eyes were leaking now. The man's hand swung around, catching Denarius in the mouth and splitting his lip. Denarius sprawled on his back, leaves and needles crunching beneath him. He looked up in time to see the revolver swinging around to point at his face.

"Goddamn nig—" Wild Bob began before the revolver was flipping away from his exploding hand in a mist of red and pink, chunks of meat and bone spraying in all directions, leaving only a ragged stump with the bottom fifth of the man's palm the only evidence he'd had a hand there at all a moment before.

The look in Wild Bob's eyes was one of absolutes. Absolute confusion. Absolute pain. Absolute horror. A high-pitched squeal was hissing from the man's mouth now—one Denarius would not have thought possible for a grown man to achieve—and his one remaining hand was gripping the wrist beneath the jetting stump.

Denarius scrambled back on his ass as Wild Bob collapsed to the ground, writhing in pain and panic, the squeal an ever-present music. Tears flowed from the man's terror-filled eyes and Denarius could see the man had lost all reason, gone mad in an instant at the loss of his extremity.

A shadow moved and Denarius looked up to see a man materialize from the gloom. He was tall and broad, and wore a wide-brimmed hat. He was a white man, but Denarius did not fear him, though the man's face was fierce and hard. He wore a long coat which stopped just beneath his knees, and in his hands were one of those repeater rifles he'd heard the Confederate boys call *'them damn Yankee rifles you can load on Sunday and fire all week'*. Only this one was a newer model, not like the ones he'd seen during the war.

"Mister," the man spoke as he approached, flipping the lever out on his rifle and ejecting a round, then slamming it back in place. "You alright?"

Denarius could only stare at the man, his lips

trembling in awe. The man got to where Wild Bob lay squirming and hissing on the ground, looked down at the injured man, then back to Denarius.

"Mister?" he asked. His tone was hard, but not cruel. Curious, perhaps.

Denarius dug around and found his voice. "Y-yes, suh," he said. "I-I's alright, suh. Th-thank you, suh. You done saved my life. I don't know what I'da done if you ain't come along when you did."

The man only nodded and looked back down to Wild Bob's writhing figure. Blood was pooled into a muddy lake all around him, the leaves and pine needles floating like lilies and logs in a debris filled river.

"I hear this man correct?" the man said, pointing to Wild Bob with the barrel of his rifle. "They's gonna make a eunuch out of you?"

The man looked up after his question, a not quite confused expression on his face. Denarius nodded.

"Y-yes, suh, you heard 'em right. They's bad men. Come to my house two days ago and took me. I managed to hide my wife and boy 'neath the house before they come in. They took me and was headed down Pittsburg way. They's a man there likes to buy negro parts."

The man regarded him for a long moment, his face scrunching in disgust.

"That's right awful, mister," the man said, a hint of sympathy in his voice. "Why would the law allow such a thing to go on?"

"I's only three-fifths a man, suh. They don't see us the same as white folk. We hardly more than animals to them."

The man's head cocked to one side and his eyes squinted.

"You look like *all* of a man to me, mister. I suppose that's not the universal opinion 'round here, though."

He looked back down to Wild Bob.

"You aim to take this man's pecker off and sell it, were ya?" he said and nudged Wild Bob with the barrel of his rifle. "That your goal, to take a fellow human being's manhood off and sell it for coin?"

Wild Bob only writhed and moaned, his face and beard now coated crimson from the spray.

The man shook his head and returned his gaze to Denarius.

"Name's James Dee, mister," he said and tipped his hat with his free hand. "I'm glad I's on the trail here and seen what was happening when I did. Might've gone poorly for you otherwise."

Denarius smiled briefly and a bark of laughter escaped him, though he thought it absurd.

"You and me both, mister!" he said. "I owe you my life. I aim to repay the favor."

The man waved a hand in the air. "Think nothing of it. I'm headed to Dust, anyhow, and you say you've got a family. You get back to them."

Denarius scrambled to his feet then and dusted off his britches.

"No, suh," he said, shaking his head. "I'm a Christian man and I believe God put you in my path this day. If you're heading to . . . to Dust . . . well, suh, then so is I, least until I can repay the debt."

"Mister, you don't know—"

"I know it's the right thing to do, repay a kindness

for a kindness. And I'm handy, too. I can shoe horses, cook up a mean pot of stew, and I'm not a bad shot, neither. And the name's Denarius, suh. Denarius King."

The man named James Dee regarded him for a long moment, his hard eyes narrow, then he nodded.

"Alright, Denarius King," he said. "You don't know what you're getting into, but I can see you're a man of conviction. I won't stop you, and I'd be much obliged for a pot of stew tonight. I've got squirrel and rabbit back at my camp. Can you work with that?"

Denarius laughed so hard he doubled over, slapping his knee before coming back up.

"Suh, you ain't never *had* stew like I'm gonna make for you tonight. My name's King, and we gonna eat like one!"

James smiled at him and nodded. "Fair enough. Why don't you pick one of them horses for yourself and we'll head back to camp."

"Yes, suh," Denarius said and made his way to the horses before stopping and turning back to James. "W-what about him?"

He pointed to the still moaning and crying Wild Bob.

James looked down at the man for a moment, then said, "Him? I don't reckon a eunuch's gonna cause us no harm."

He swung the barrel to the man's crotch and blew his balls off in a shower of blood. The high-pitched squeal seemed like a deep bass note when compared to the song Wild Bob now sung, his good hand and stump both reaching for his now sexless groin.

Denarius gulped audibly as he and the man called James Dee watched Wild Bob bleed to death.

7

DENARIUS HADN'T BEEN lying about his abilities with the stew. James couldn't remember the last time he'd eaten so well, certainly in camp. He lay back with his head on his saddle, hat to his side, picking at his fingernails with a knife. Denarius was across the fire from him, staring at him with a curious look in his dark eyes as the flames cast lapping shadows across his features.

"What's on your mind, Denarius?" James said, not looking up from his work with the knife.

He sensed rather than saw Denarius shrug.

"I's just curious, suh," the black man said. "What's in this place you headed called Dust? I ain't never heard of the place before, and I's lived 'round here my whole life, least far back as I can remember."

James finished with his fingernails and drove the blade of his knife into the ground next to him before looking across the fire to his new friend.

"Dust is . . . " he began and trailed off, trying to decide on what exactly to tell the man. "Well, Dust is a bad place. Built on bad ground. There's something there that needs dispatching, let's put it that way."

"Some*thing*, suh?" Denarius asked. "Not some*one*?"

James nodded. "That's right. Though I suspect the residents of Dust may have a vested interest in keeping this something safe. I expect they won't take too kindly to my meaning to dispatch it outright. Is what it is, I suppose."

"What is it?"

"What's what, Denarius?"

"The thing, suh. What is it in Dust you aim to dispatch? And how come I never heard of this town before now?"

James smiled and looked into the fire for a few moments before answering. There was so much this man wouldn't understand, wouldn't be *capable* of understanding. But James had judged him to be a decent fellow, and he was coming along to help James, so he decided the man deserved the truth. At least the closest approximation of it James could deliver, anyway.

"I'm from around these parts as well, Denarius," James began, sitting up and resting his elbows on his knees. "But I'm also not. Everything is familiar and totally foreign all at once. I know that's hard to understand, but I don't suspect I can make it much clearer. Sometimes I have a hard time wrapping my own head around it. But it's real. I come nearly full circle here from where I began. You see, I was a lawman once upon a time."

"A lawman, you say?"

James nodded. "Yessir, I do say. I was a chief, as a matter of fact, though you'd more likely think of it as a Sheriff or a Marshall, I suspect. Sheriffs are different there, though we've still got 'em. Anyhow, there was this . . . *thing* came to my town. Wasn't no human. It was a threat. A *big* threat. Could've ended the world, if you can believe that. Hell, I suspect you don't, but it's the truth."

Denarius looked offended. "I ain't called you no liar, mister. Until you prove yourself dishonest to me, I'm taking you at your word."

James looked at the man through the flames and nodded to him, the faintest hint of a smile playing at the corners of his mouth.

"Alright, Denarius. I appreciate that."

Denarius nodded. "So this thing could have ended the world, you say?"

James nodded again. "That's right. You see, it was a real-life monster. That's no lie. And the only way I could stop it, took me out of my town and out of my world. I ended up adrift in this . . . *other* place. I come to call it the *Void* in time, because there just wasn't nothing there. It was *void* of anything. Well, almost anything, that is. There were these people there. And not really people, per se, but *Others*. They live there, just on the outside of everything we can see and feel and touch. I called them the *Others*. And I learned from them that there are threats to our world and many others. Gods, you might call them, but not *the* God. They're powerful, monstrous things. Their only purpose seems to be to destroy. Destroy whole worlds and peoples. And because of that, I decided I had to rid the universe of them. I been seeing to that now going on two decades."

Denarius squinted at him through the fire, soaking in the information. James could tell the man was confused, had questions. But he didn't ask them. James went on.

"I can do things, Denarius. Crazy things. Maybe *the* God gave me the ability, maybe evolution allowed it to develop in me for some reason. I don't know. All I know is I can do these things and it makes it so I can do away with these gods. And I aim to do just that in Dust. The Others told me about all the different gods out there, and I'm on a mission to kill 'em all."

"Killing *gods*?" Denarius asked and uttered a soft chuckle. "Mister, that beats all I ever heard."

"Yeah," James said and tossed a shard of fingernail into the fire. "Somebody's gotta do it, I reckon. May as well be me. That way maybe Joanna can live in peace."

"Joanna your wife, mister?" Denarius asked, his eyes perking up.

James shook his head. "Daughter. She's back . . . where I come from. With her mother and my best friend. I checked in on them for a while when I could, though they didn't know it and it's been some time since I've been able to. But she's safe. For now, anyway."

Denarius nodded and looked about the camp as though searching for something to say.

He found it.

"What abilities?"

James looked at him a moment before realizing what he was referring to, then smiled.

"Oh, little of this, little of that."

Denarius shook his head and laughed.

"Naw, suh. You don't tell a man something like that and not show him what you speaking of. I may be three-fifths a man, but you *five*-fifths out your damn mind you think you ain't about to show me what you talking about."

They shared a laugh at this, a genuine and deep belly laugh. James couldn't remember the last time he'd had a laugh like that. It felt good.

Finally, he nodded.

"You still got that knife?" James asked.

Denarius's grin turned confused, but still amused.

"Yes suh, I do."

"Hold it up."

Denarius stared at him a moment longer, blinking several times, then reached for the knife next to him on the ground. He held it up, still grinning.

It was suddenly jerked from his hand as though an invisible force had yanked it free. He watched in stunned awe as it sailed across the fire, the now cleaned blade winking in the firelight.

There was a clap as the handle slapped into James's hand. Denarius's mouth hung agape in stunned awe.

"D-did you . . . " Denarius started. "Was that—"

"Yes sir, Mr. King," James said as the flames twinkled in his eyes. "And that ain't the half of it."

Denarius's face split into a wide grin.

8

"YOU HUNGRY, GEAR?" Quentin asked from the inky shadows deep in the woods. Dreary paid him no mind as he watched through his collapsible telescope at the distant fire flickering through the trees.

The moon was a bone scythe in dark sky, sparkling diamonds of stars glittering about in brilliant starkness all above them. But they were not focusing on the beauty of the night above the trees, nor could they have fully appreciated the spectacle from their current vantage. It was late now, and though Dust was a town of near myth, Dreary knew they were close now. So very close. And the gunman Dee was leading them right to it.

His beard malformed into a savage grin.

"Gear?" Quentin repeated, reaching a hand out to touch his boss's arm. "Are you—"

"I'll appreciate you respecting my personal space, Quentin," Dreary said, never taking his eye from the scope.

Quentin paused, his hand only a few inches from Dreary's arm, and withdrew.

"Sorry, Gear," Quentin said. "I was about to fire up some logs and heat the beans."

"You'll do no such thing!" Dreary hissed, finally turning from his scope and glaring at Quentin through the gloom. "We're much too close now to give our position away with your deplorable appetite. Eat them cold or not at all."

Despite the shadows, Quentin's face could be seen well enough to make out the scrunch of displeasure which contorted it.

"Ah, Gear, them beans ain't no good uncooked!"

"Then abstain," Dreary spoke indifferently.

Quentin started to protest further when both Avery and Bonham put a hand each on his arms, shaking their heads. He sighed harshly and sat back against the fallen log behind him and crossed his arms like a petulant child.

"I can appreciate the hungers of a man, dear Quentin," Dreary said, lowering the scope but not collapsing it. "I have appetites of my own. In fact, it is one such appetite which directs this very scene we find ourselves in now."

Dreary turned to face his three companions in the dark. His eyes blazed in the sparse moonlight.

"Do you men really understand what awaits us in Dust?" he asked, looking at their silhouettes in turn.

None of them answered.

Dreary reached into his rucksack and produced a leather-bound book, tied closed with a string on the front. He held it up in the gloom for them to see in a shaft of light through the trees.

"It's all here," he said, nodding toward the book. "The legend of the Elders."

"Elders?" Avery asked, his pitch a note too high. "Like old folks?"

Dreary sighed and shook his head slowly.

"No, Avery, not like old people. *The* Elders. The ancients. I'm talking about *gods*."

"Oh," Avery said as though some great epiphany had just dawned on him. "Like the burning bush and that feller on the cross, then."

He wasn't asking a question this time, but stating it as though it were fact, some infallible bit of information he'd just unearthed.

Dreary sighed and lowered the book. "No, I'm afraid you're wrong again. I'm not talking about religion and folk tales. This isn't a Bible in my hands. It's a record. A record of the ancient gods, the ones that live outside of our plane of existence, but just beneath the surface. They are awesome and fearsome beings, powerful beyond your wildest imagination. You cannot *fathom* the power of these creatures."

Quentin sat forward, draping his arms across his knees.

"What's any of this bullshit got to do with my dinner?" he asked, that petulant tone still saturating his words.

Dreary smiled in the dark. "Quentin, that man yonder through the woods is leading us straight to the town of Dust, a town shrouded in mystery and shadows. But it isn't the *town* I'm after. No sir. It's what the town is *hiding* I aim to find. The relic of another time. Another plane of existence. It's shown up throughout history in various places across the globe according to the texts I have here. In ancient Egypt and Mesopotamia. Babylon. More recently in the Southern Americas."

The three silhouettes stared at him in the darkness. Only Bonham seemed disinterested.

"I still don't see what any of that has to do with—"

"It's the relic of *N'yea'thuul*, you idiot!" Dreary cut him off with a hiss, a furious tone in his whisper. "The god of destruction. And I'm much too close now to let you give our position away to our friend, Mr. James Dee, because your tummy is growling!"

"Gear," a flat voice came through, void of emotion. It was Bonham. Dreary was startled by the man's voice, not because it was fearsome, but because the man rarely spoke.

Dreary turned his head to the man. "Yes, Mr. Bonham?"

Bonham leaned forward himself, fussing with something in his hands. Dreary assumed he was picking his nails with his knife, though he couldn't confirm this visually.

"Ain't this fella—this Mr. James—ain't he after the same thing as you?"

A long silence followed the question as Dreary sat back, mulling the question over. Finally, he spoke in a quiet tone.

"Mr. James Dee *is* after the relic of *N'yea'thuul*, yes. But he isn't after what *I'm* after. Our friend Mr. James will have to suffer an untimely death, I'm afraid, though his guidance to our treasure is greatly appreciated. Yet, it must be so. I aim to *harness* the power of the relic. Mr. James aims to destroy it. We cannot allow that. But timing is everything, dear fellows. Timing is *everything*."

"S-so we get into Dust, then we smoke the son of a bitch and find this re-lick? That it?" Quentin asked.

"It's *relic*, my dear boy, and yes, that's about the size of it," Dreary replied. "But I've no desire to cross arms with the man headlong. He's an accomplished gunslinger and rumored to be a master of magic as well. His assassination will be best accomplished through stealth and distance."

The men nodded slowly, their moist eyes glinting in the moonlight. The crickets sang in the night as the four men fell into a long, contemplative silence. Finally, Quentin asked a final question.

"Gear, when we find this, uh, *rellick*," he said, drawing the word out, "what do you aim to do with it, exactly?"

Dreary smiled and turned back to the distant, flickering fire through the trees and raised the scope to his eye once more.

"Why, my dear Quentin," he said in a low voice which was almost a growl, "I shall join the ranks of the divine."

He slammed the scope closed.

9

" . . . ET HER TO . . . ELIC. "

Bits and pieces of words drifted to her through the murk of her mind as she became aware of a driving pain in her skull. She tried opening her eyes, but all she was able to make out were constellations of black stars and planets orbiting invisible suns and the sensation caused her gorge to rise. She let her eyes drift closed again as she strained to listen to the words of the man which still drifted in and out around the thrumming pain in her skull.

" . . . take the boy to . . . eet back at the temp . . . "

She couldn't focus. The pain was searing and horrific. What was even more horrific was the seeming blankness in her mind as to what was going on. She began searching for memories, anything that would shed light on what was happening to her. For a frightening moment, she realized she didn't even know how she knew what a memory *was*, let alone how to locate one within her brain. Her heart began to race and she felt a tingling sensation wash over her from the base of her neck down to her thighs, spreading to her fingertips like pricking tacks.

My God, she thought. *Oh, my God, what's*

happening? Where am I? Who *am I?*

Fresh panic threatened to seize within her at the advent of her own thoughts. *Who* was she? How could she not know who she was? How could she not know what was happening? Why couldn't she remember anything and why was her head hurting so much and her vision so blur—

A sharp pain smacked the back of her already pounding skull and she winced involuntarily. She tried opening her eyes once more and found the constellations still there, but now swirling only in the periphery of her vision. It was dark out, though she thought she could see a pink kiss rising above the tree line announcing the onset of dawn.

Dawn is morning, she thought. *Dawn is when the sun rises in the morning.*

That was something. Some sort of memory. Or understanding, at the very least. But this didn't answer the question of what was happening to her. She blinked her eyes some more to clear them.

Three sharp raps to the back of her skull that smarted fiercely and caused her to wince again brought her further out of the murk. She glanced down and realized she was being dragged by . . . by a . . .

She couldn't make it out. The darkness was closing in once more as she was pulled through a doorway. Sharp splinters snagged at her dress and pricked the soft flesh of her arms which lolled above her head. She was being taken into a building or a house of some kind. That was why the faint pink light had faded back to a cloak of deep gray, edging on black.

Whatever it was that had been dragging her

stopped and she felt her feet drop to the floor, the impact making a loud *thud* on the planks. The heels of her feet ached and her head throbbed in unison with her heartbeat.

She moaned.

Whatever had been dragging her moved in the shadows, an inky creature in the dark, indistinguishable aside from its movements. She became aware of a deep, bubbling sound, of a strange rasping of breath.

Of *clicking* sounds.

Something skittered in the darkness beyond sight, like too many feet lightly tiptoeing on the wooden planks of the floor. The bubbling, rasping, clicking sounds continued. She began to try and move, first up on her elbows, then to her side. She snaked a hand around to the back of her head and felt the knot there. It was an angry thing, hot and swollen, and her touch upon it neared on agony.

Another wince and her hand came away and joined her other, palm down on the floor. She took deep breaths, trying to steady her ever rising gorge. Sharply through the nose, long and slow past her lips. After a few moments, the nausea passed again and she managed to roll herself over onto her knees.

"W-what's going on?" she asked, her voice feeble in the dark space. She could hear the skittering thing moving and breathing and clicking and . . .

She tried not to focus on the sounds. They weren't natural. She wasn't sure how she knew what natural was when she couldn't even manage to land on her name or what had happened or how she'd gotten here. But she knew. Instinctively, she knew.

Something bred into her through millions of years. Something deep within her, far in the back of her ancient lizard brain which remained largely inactive except when danger lurked.

And she was convinced it lurked now.

"I-I don't—"

"Sssssiiillllleeeeeeennnnnccce," a sickening voice slithered into her ears from the abyss all around her, chilling her blood in place.

Her spine rippled and gooseflesh erupted over back and arms. Even her buttocks rippled with the stuff. Her eyes were wide in the gloom, though she realized she could see just a bit more than she had before. At first, she thought her eyes were adjusting to the dark, but then she saw the thin reams of light cutting through the outer edge of a pair of shuttered windows across the room. The sun was rising outside.

Windows, she thought. *Windows. Sunlight. You know these things, woman! And you're a woman! Who are you? Think!*

"Who are you?" she asked the voice in the dark as she made her way onto shaky legs. "What is thi—"

A memory flared in her mind. She was beneath a house, holding someone close to her chest. It was a boy. A young boy. Was he *her* boy?

Yes. She knew that like she knew what a window was and what sunlight was. They were beneath a house, and men were screaming above. Someone was hurt and being dragged over the planks above them and out the door. The boy was crying and she was desperately trying to shush him, to keep him quiet because the bad men were there, the *very* bad men, and if they heard him, they would be taken too.

"*Nigger!*" she recalled one of the men's voices shouting above them. "*Y'all's parts bring a high price! You got you a black bitch around here, boy? Got a little coal baby stashed somewhere?*"

It was coming back to her. The very bad men hurting someone above where she and the boy hid. *Her* boy.

"*I ain't gots nobody, suh!*" a new voice whimpered. The voice of someone she knew. Someone she . . .

She loved them. Whoever it was, she *loved* them and the boy wasn't just hers, he was *theirs*. The fruit of their love. Her . . . he was her . . .

Husband.

"*I's all alone here, suh, I tells ya the truth!*" the man whom she loved was saying.

He was lying. Lying to save her and the boy. What was his name? What was the boy's name?

What was her na—

"*Maaaaarrrrrrllllllleeeeennnnnaaaa,*" the slithering, satanic voice hissed from the gloom, ripping her from her memories.

Her head jerked in the direction of the sound, the motion causing her vision to swirl and she stumbled a step before recovering. She recognized the name. She'd *responded* to the name, not just the voice. It was as if she'd been addressed by whatever abomination had dragged her into this terrible place.

It was *her* name.

"Marlena," she repeated her name, as though trying it on for the first time. But she immediately felt completely at home and familiar with it. It was as much a part of her as her arm.

"*Yyyyeeeeeeeessssssssss,*" the skittering thing said as its light and terrifying footfalls seemed to echo about the room, its bubbling, clicking, rasping breath now coupled with a low growl. *"You are highly favored to receive the honor of feeding the Elderrrrrrrr."*

The thing's word dragged on for a maddeningly long time before finally drifting into silence. Her eyes were more focused now and she looked about the room she was in. It had a familiar feel, but felt all wrong at the same time. She could make out rows of seating with an aisle in the center, and she realized she stood at the back of what seemed to be a church. It wasn't unlike her own church where she and her husband worshipped with their boy—*Martin, that was his name!*—on Sundays. Only, the front of the sanctuary was all wrong. Instead of a lectern, there was some sort of strange altar. Even this shouldn't have seemed out of place, but the thing was unlike any altar she'd ever seen, and her memories were rushing back to her in force now. The altar was quite large, more than ten feet on a side, and it seemed to be a perfect cube.

"What is this place?" Marlena asked, turning her gaze to the gloom where she'd last heard the skittering thing speak. Where she could hear its terrible clicking and bubbling growl.

She heard the thing laugh, and as it did, it moved. The skittering sounds of its feet—too many feet, she decided—moved in front of one of the windows with the light streaming in around the edges of its shuttered surface. She thought she could make out the rough shape of a man in the middle, the arms and legs dangling like limp noodles, but that was where all similarity with humanity ended. There were arching, knuckled things coming from either end of the shape, and while she couldn't be sure in the dark, she thought they were protruding from the head and . . . *anus?*

She gasped as her hand clasped over her mouth. Insanely, she remembered clambering out from beneath the house with Martin, some time after the very bad men had taken her husband, and being clubbed in the back of the head. All was black after that.

Until now.

"Thiiiiiiisssssssss is the temple of N'yea'thuullllll."

There was a wet, smacking sound and she could just make out a crimson sphere that seemed to rise up from the middle of the skittering thing. When the wet, smacking sound made its encore, she finally made out what the sphere was.

It was a blinking, red eye. She screamed.

10

LIGHT TRICKLED IN through the thinning treetops as James and Denarius sauntered along. Dawn was coming on, though the sky was overcast with gray clouds, threatening a coming storm. The air smelled of pine and moisture, the temperature comfortable despite the warmth of the season as the breeze whisked through the trees, carrying the cool air past them like a chilling balm.

Their horses whinnied and snorted, seeming to slow despite the urgings of James and Denarius. Something up ahead wasn't sitting right with them and they were reluctantly obedient to continue on. The soft *clop-ah-dah-clop-ah-dah* of their hoof falls drummed in the music of the early morning birds and crawling things.

Up ahead, James spied what seemed to be the mouth of the trail. The trees widened, thinning ever more, and there was a slight rise. Beyond it he could just make out the top of what looked like a roof, but the grade hid the rest.

"Looks like we've found Dust, Denarius," James said as he pulled on the reins to halt his steed. Denarius did the same. The horses seemed all too anxious to stop.

"I'll be a son of a gun," Denarius said, using his hand as a visor over his eyes to block the gray morning light. "So it *is* a real place."

James gave him a sidelong look.

"Did you doubt me, friend?" he asked, a sly grin parting his lips.

Denarius arched his back straight and adjusted himself in his saddle, shaking his head and waving a hand.

"Now, now, I ain't said that, Mr. James. I ain't said that at all. I just . . . well, hell, with all you done told me and showed me last night, I . . . it's just a lot to process all at once. A man needs time to digest that kind of information."

James nodded and squinted his eyes as he peered back toward the outskirts of Dust, remembering all he'd shown and told Denarius the previous night. He'd shown him first how he was able to manipulate objects with the power of his will. Even showed him how he was able to come to this time in history seven years prior. Only shown, not taken Denarius along for a demonstration. Still, the man's mind had been nearly blown clear of his skull, his wide eyes and slack-jawed mouth a testament to his astonishment.

He'd told Denarius of how he'd moved from a place—or more properly described as a *world*—to the middle of the Chisolm Trail in a town called Duncan, in the middle of a territory that would soon be known as the state of Oklahoma, within the next thirty years or so. Little of this had made sense to Denarius, who had listened on in awe as James described stumbling into a jail and meeting a gentleman named Karl Beck who'd pointed him south toward Texas.

Then had come the long tale of James's journey, always hunting the elusive town of Dust, and later hearing of a man named Dreary who had moved into the area, apparently in search of the same place.

"I aim to find Dust and kill what's there," James had told Denarius as they stared into the campfire. "The elder gods are killers. Destroyers. All throughout the universe, throughout *all* universes, these things are dormant. Sleeping. Waiting to be awakened. For willing servants to usher them out of their banishment. That's one thing I'll give the *real* God, he put them away. But there are forces working against Him, and they placed these markers throughout the cosmos."

He had gestured up to the sky and they had both looked up to the stars.

"Everywhere you see up there, Denarius, all over, there are other worlds, other civilizations. Most are like us, just trying to make the best of what they have. Some are more malevolent. But *all* of the elder gods are right on the outskirts of their reality. Most of them don't even know it. But there are some who do, who seek to find the markers and make soldiers for the elders. Once they amass enough soldiers, their aim is to trigger the marker and call the elders forward. They're so mad with the lust for power, they're calling their own destruction and annihilation forth. Most of them know it, too. But that's why I think God gave me these gifts . . . "

James had held his hand out to the air and one of his revolvers had slapped into his hand. Then he casually cocked the hammer and reseated it gently.

"To find these gods. And kill them."

"And this Dreary fella," Denarius had asked in a shaky tone, "he one of them fools tryin' to call forth this elder god, uh, what was its name again?"

"N'yea'thuul," James had said and nodded. "And yes, Denarius, he is. I've been aiming to find him and put him down before he had a chance to find Dust before I did. Now, I'm so damn close, all I really need to do is get into Dust and kill the soldiers. Then I can banish the marker and Dreary can do what he likes. He won't be able to call the elder forth."

Now, as James stared at the tip of the roof in the distance, he wondered if that had been a sound plan, after all. Dreary was dangerous. Dreary had killed, or facilitated the killing of, many men. Women and children, too. If there was information to be gained, it didn't matter to him the obstacle before in his path. He would put it down. A man like that had no business living.

But, as James dismounted his horse and leaned sharply to stretch his back, he supposed he wasn't too far off from being the same sort of man Dreary was. In reality, wasn't the only actual difference between them the *reason* for finding the marker?

He thought so, but decided it would have to be enough.

You have a pure heart, Agatha Dupree had said. *But you're not a good man. Perhaps you were once.*

He shook off the thoughts and led his horse to an oak and tied off the reins. Denarius was doing likewise.

"I want to give you one last chance to scurry on back to your family," James said as he pulled his repeater from the sheath on his saddle and dropped it into another which rested across his back. "This here's my fight, not yours."

Denarius held up a hand.

"I appreciate your saying so, Mr. James, but I owe you a debt, whether you recognize it or not. I made sure my family was safe before them bad men got to me. They'll be safe when I return."

James stared hard at the man for a long moment. He regarded him with equal parts respect and pity. He was obviously a man of deep moral conviction, but he was also a man who, while James had explained many things to him, still didn't *really* understand what they were walking into.

"Alright, then," James said and nodded. He decided not to press the issue further. If the stories about Dust turned out to be accurate, the poor bastard would see for himself soon enough. Plenty of time to turn tail and run then.

James began moving toward town, but stopped when he felt Denarius's hand on his arm. He turned and faced him, his new friend's face a shade lighter than it had been up to now.

"You have an extra shooter, suh?" Denarius asked, swallowing hard. "I aim to help you out, but I ain't gonna be much good without some iron to toss."

James blinked a few times, thinking. He had both his revolvers on him and his rifle slung across his back. His only other weapon was the large knife sheathed in his belt at the base of his back. Well, other than . . .

"I *do* have one other weapon," he said, moving to his saddle bag. "But the ammunition is limited. In any case, you're welcome to use it so long as you mind the recoil and don't hit me with it."

Denarius laughed, throwing his head back as James dug out the revolver.

"Mr. James, I can handle the recoil on anything you got just fine, I assure ya!"

James smiled as he pulled the gun from the bag and held it out to Denarius.

"Don't be so sure, friend."

Denarius's face clouded with confusion as he accepted the firearm in cradling hands, holding the weapon as if it were a religious relic. His eyes darted all over it as he turned it over in his hands, marveling at the craftsmanship and what James assumed to be confoundment at the near alien nature of the thing.

"W-what is . . . " Denarius started and then gulped, his throat clicking. "Just what in the blue hell is *this?*"

He held the revolver up between them.

James chuckled. "That there, my new friend, is a Smith & Wesson Performance Center Pro Series Model 686. Fires the .357 Magnum round. That's one hell of a caliber. It screams like a shrieking demon and bucks like a mule. But if you aim it halfway decent, it's a one and done kind of weapon."

Denarius's confusion only seemed to deepen.

"A three-fifty-seven?" Denarius exclaimed in confused astonishment. "I heard of plenty of calibers, but I ain't never—"

"And you likely won't," James said, cutting him off and handing him a fistful of shells. Denarius held one up, his jaw dredging new depths beneath his face. "It hasn't been invented yet. Hell, it's a longer and meaner version of the .38 Special, and even *that* ain't been invented yet. But never mind all that. All you need to know is it's powerful as hell, and you need to hang on when you fire it. And fire it sparingly, as I said, I don't have too many rounds for it."

He fished around in his saddle bag and produced some more shells and handed them to Denarius, who shoved them into his pocket. Denarius fumbled with a lever on the side and the whole cylinder rolled out to one side, exposing six empty chambers.

"I'll be a son of a gun," Denarius was muttering, still in awe. But he was thumbing rounds into the chambers and when he had it full, he slammed the cylinder back into the housing of the gun. His hand flexed on it a few times, his fingers exploring the grip.

"Like the feel of it, do ya?" James asked as they began to make their way up the grade to a ridge overlooking Dust.

"Yes, suh, I sure do!" Denarius exclaimed.

James nodded. "Thought you might. It's a fine weapon. It's the one I carried as a lawman where I'm from. I'd carry it still if there were ammunition for it to come by. Ain't none, though, and won't be for a lot of years yet, I'm afraid."

He trailed off as he hunched down, climbing the ridge, and realized Denarius was staring at him.

"What is it, Denarius?"

His new friend's face parted in an astonished grin and his head shook.

"Mr. James, suh, you ain't crazy a'tall, is ya?" Denarius asked.

James laughed and pulled his rifle from his back.

"Sometimes, Denarius, I wish I were."

He chambered a round.

11

DREARY LOOKED OUT over the landscape below. The gray light from the overcast sky shed a gloom over the town, though he believed the town of Dust would be a gloomy sight in any lighting. The dirt streets were a bland shade of maroon from the iron ore clay in the ground, and the buildings were sparse and in disrepair. At the end of the main street, which slinked arrow straight up the town's center, stood a large building with a spire sporting some sort of coiling spiral symbol at its top jutting to the sky above its large double entry doors. Behind it lay a sprawling lake, one seemingly as hidden from public knowledge as the town itself. The gray light twinkled off the surface as a soft breeze created rippling waves across its shimmering top, which bordered three sides of the town.

The buildings between the one with the spire—*was it a church?*—were in far worse disrepair than it. Windows were missing entirely or reached out like claws in their frames, doors hung open, some at odd angles, others gone entirely. Not a single roof in all the town seemed sound enough to keep water out. In fact, the whole place looked like a ghost town, as though the whole of the people had packed up and left one day, eager to flee.

Yet, there *were* signs of life all the same. A stable near what Dreary assumed to be an old saloon held half a dozen horses which were grazing on piles of hay and slurping water from troughs. Behind the main street some distance there was a ranch house on the shore of the lake, smoke pluming from its chimney, and several cows grazing the field surrounding it, along with a pair of goats and a swath of chickens, their distant clucks reaching their ears like faint chokes.

But not a soul was on the streets. This wasn't all that odd, he surmised. It *was* only just past dawn. Likely the town was still sleeping. Though, despite the few houses he could see at the outskirts and butting up against the lake, he wondered what kind of people would live in a town such as this, so cut off from the world and society. But he knew the answer to this and smiled broadly.

A town building the army of N'yea'thuul.

Dreary aimed his telescope to his left and down the ridge a way to where James Dee and his new friend were perched. James had his rifle out, the black man lying prone next to him. Both had their eyes pinned to the town, searching it over much as he'd been doing a moment ago. Surveying the territory. Dreary smiled once more as he collapsed his telescope and put it away. Then he patted Mr. Bonham on the shoulder. The big man turned and looked to him, a long-barreled repeater in his hands, not unlike the one James Dee was sporting.

Dreary leaned in and whispered so as not to send his words echoing in valley of the town.

"I believe our friend Mr. Dee has outlived his usefulness," Dreary said, his eyes alight with anticipation. "See that he and the negro are dispatched without any fuss. Start with Dee."

Bonham made the closest approximation to a grin the man was capable of and gave a nearly imperceptible nod. Then he crawled on his belly to the edge of a rock and cradled the rifle up to his shoulder. Dreary crept up beside him, lightning tingling in his fingertips. He wanted to watch James Dee's head pop like a pulsating sore, to see the gray pus of his brains scatter the rocks beside the man. For years, he'd managed to stay just a step ahead of James Dee, the man on a mission to destroy the gods and snatch from Dreary his destiny of divinity. And now he had the drop on the man. He would savor the moment.

The hammer of Bonham's repeater clicked as it was cocked into place, a satisfying ratcheting sound which sent pleasuring shivers up Dreary's spine. Bonham exhaled slowly, resting his cheek on the butt of the weapon, squinting down the site with one eye.

Movement on the other side of James and his companion caused Dreary to nearly cry out as his hand shot down to the rifle and his thumb was pinched harshly as the hammer descended on it. Bonham had just pulled the trigger, but Dreary's interference had stopped the weapon from firing and caused a nasty wound to begin bleeding from his hand.

"Goddamnit, Gear!" Bonham hissed, pulling the hammer back so Dreary could remove his thumb. "What in hell'd you do that for?"

Dreary stuck the side of his bleeding thumb into

his mouth, sucking at the coppery sweetness of his blood, and pointed with his other hand.

"There."

Bonham's eyes followed Dreary's directions and widened when they fell upon three men stepping out of the trees behind James and the black man.

"I'll be dipped in shit," Bonham said, almost gasping. "Where the hell did—"

"From the town," Dreary said as he pulled his thumb from his mouth, now awash with his own blood, and began to wrap it in a cloth. "Men from the town. I dare not move on Dee with them right there. If one gets away before we can get into town, I might never get to my treasure. And . . . "

Dreary trailed off, his face splitting into another maliciously broad smile.

"And what, Gear?" Quentin asked as he and Avery sidled up next to them.

Dreary's piercing gaze bore into the scene unfolding below them, his teeth shimmering in the gray light.

"Mr. James Dee might just get served up to N'yea'thuul," he said, a madness blazing in his eyes. "And, *oh*, what sweet irony that would be. These men are doing our job for us."

They began making their way down the ridge toward Dust.

PART III:

WELCOME TO DUST

12

DENARIUS HEARD THE *shuck-shuck* of the repeater a half-second before he saw the men stepping from the woods. His hand jerked toward the crazy weapon from the future in his waistband on instinct, but stopped short when he saw the barrel of the repeater trained on them. The other two men on either side of the repeater man had revolvers drawn, their faces dirty and coated in a week's worth of whiskers.

He raised his hands as he got to his knees.

"The hell business you boys got here?" the one with the repeater asked, though his tone did not convey malice. Instead, it seemed almost defeated, as though he were being forced into a position he had no desire to be in. The look on his face, the deep ridges of concern and sorrow, bore this out.

The look on the other two men's faces did not seem likewise afflicted.

"Gentlemen," James said, raising his hands and leaving his repeater where it lay. "I believe you've found us in an awkward position here."

Grunts from the two revolver men, a twitching eye and quivering lip from the man with the repeater.

"Perhaps so," repeater man said. "But this town don't take kindly to visitors. This here's a private place, and we mean to keep it such. I'm sorry, but you're going to have to come with us. The Proprietor will have to decide what's to be done with ya."

Denarius's gaze flicked from the men to James for just a second, then back again.

"Forgive me, suh," Denarius said, "but you said the *Proprietor?* Who is—"

"You best keep them blue gums shut, nigger!" the revolver man to the left of repeater said. "Ain't no one said a goddamn thing to you!"

Denarius's jaw clenched tight and he fought to hide a scowl of fury which threatened to tear across his face. He had been raised a slave and spent the last near decade and a half considered only three-fifths a man. He was accustomed to bigotry. It was as much a constant in his life as the need to piss. Wasn't something he could get away from, nor did he expect to. He'd been called *nigger* and *spook* and *coon* more times now than there were calculable numbers. But it wasn't the use of the slur that made him angry now. What infuriated him was the rudeness of the man's behavior. Rudeness was uncalled for. He'd been called these same names and worse before, but without the coldly rude tone. Most men were ignorant. It was just a fact of life in these parts. It was a word. A descriptor. Derogatory, sure. But often used in ignorance, not malice. It didn't make it okay, but he could look past ignorance. He could *not*, however, look past malice.

And this man was *full* of malice.

"I see those giant lips open one more time, you'll

have a fucking hole the size of my fist right in the middle of your black face, you hear me, boy?"

Denarius met the man's gaze, glaring fiercely at him. But he said nothing. Merely nodded. Ignorant and cruel and malicious though the man may be, it didn't make him any less dangerous.

"Apologize to the man," James said flatly, his own hands still in the air to either side of his face.

The three men turned their gaze to James, and Denarius did likewise. At first, he wasn't sure who James was referring to. Did he mean for Denarius to apologize to the man with the gun? Denarius didn't take James to be like most men from these parts. He was a brutal man, but at the same time much more civilized in many respects. The idea that James would want Denarius to apologize to the malicious cowboy seemed ludicrous.

But soon Denarius realized James hadn't been referring to him at all, for his fierce gaze bore directly into the man with the revolver who'd demeaned Denarius. The man with the gun seemed to blossom with rage, his face reddening to a deep crimson, his yellowed and browned teeth exposed as his lips raised in a snarl.

"The hell you say?" the man growled, turning his gun to James.

"Everybody just hold the hell on!" the repeater man shouted, raising one hand to stay the rest. "This ain't how this is gonna go, you hear me? The Proprietor will handle this."

The revolver man and his fraternal twin both turned to glare at the repeater man.

"The Proprietor ain't here," the second revolver man said.

"But I *am*, goddammit!" repeater said. "I say what's—"

"You don't say shit!" the first revolver man said, his gun turning toward repeater.

"I *said* apologize!" James spoke in a loud and forceful tone, pulling the three men from their argument. "I won't ask a third time."

The three men seemed to jolt when James spoke, and in unison they turned to him. To a one their eyes narrowed, mouths open in bemused awe. Finally, the first revolver man spoke.

"The hell do you think you're doing, mister? We're the ones with the guns. We'll make the demands. And I ain't never apologized to no black fella, nor will I! Now, let that be the end of it."

James's head began to shake.

"You're about to not have your guns at all," he said. "You're being awfully rude to my friend here, and I don't take kindly to my friends being treated rudely. Last chance."

The revolver man began laughing then. It came in fits and starts at first, bewildered chuckles issued in short barks. Then it matured into full on guffaws of hilarity. Before long, he was doubling over and slapping at the side of his leg, his revolvered companion joining in the festivities. Only the repeater man didn't laugh. Didn't even smile. He only continued to stare at James with a confused expression.

James turned to Denarius, and Denarius could see the same coldness there he'd seen when this mysterious man of magic had blown the balls off of his kidnapper in the woods. A chill snaked down his spine.

"I warned them," James said with a shrug.

James's wrist twitched then, as though he were calling someone over with a gesture of his hand. Something scraped above and behind him, and the offending revolver man's laughter caught in his throat for a moment. He spun quickly on his heels to look behind him, as though he expected to find yet another member of their party lying in wait.

When the boulder was five feet above his face, tumbling from a higher place on the ridge, the man spoke his final word.

"Shitfire."

The repeater man and the other revolver man were showered with an obscene amount of blood and gore as the giant rock crunched their companion to a slushy mess. Meaty pulps spattered their faces and both turned, heaving and screaming. The remaining revolver man slipped on what might have been a length of intestine and fell to the ground, wincing as he made impact.

"Jesus, Mary, and Joseph!" the repeater man screamed, his eyes wide and darting around, a free hand absently swiping chunks of flesh and only God knew what else from his dripping face.

Denarius watched in stupefied awe as James then flicked both wrists and both the repeater man's rifle and the other man's revolver were torn from their hands by an invisible force and came clapping into James's outstretched hands. He was on his feet then, and Denarius was a half second behind him, moving more out of confused terror than cognitive thought. He ripped the weapon from a time yet to come from his waist band and leveled it on the remaining men as James pointed their own weapons at them.

"Now," James said, looking back and forth between the gore-soaked men, who were now trembling with shock and staring at the barrels of the guns that were trained on them. "You mentioned a Proprietor before. I think I'd like to meet this man."

The two men looked to each other and then back at James and Denarius. The man formally known as repeater to Denarius and James spoke in a wavering voice, spitting errant droplets of blood and tissue between his words.

"He ain't no man, mister."

Denarius's eyes narrowed as he glanced back at James, whom he was astonished to find was smiling.

"Well, then," James said and uttered a soft laugh, "all the more reason to make his acquaintance."

13

DREARY HAD MOVED his men further down the ridge after the three men had come out of the woods on Dee and the black man. They were in the trees now, not ten feet from a street on the edge of Dust, quietly watching and appraising the situation. He'd half expected a few gunshots to echo off the rocky ridge and out over the lake beyond town, but none had come. Aside from what sounded like a falling rock off in the distance, there had been nothing.

"What's the plan, Gear?" Quentin asked in a whisper, his eyes peeled wide and looking up and down the street. They saw no one.

"The plan is to get to that church across town, just in front of the lake," Dreary said, indicating the direction with a nod of his head. "That'll be where the marker is. If I've any luck on my side yet, I'll find a suitable sacrifice between here and there."

Quentin's eyes narrowed a bit as he glanced to Dreary and then back to the street.

"What's this about sacrifice?" he asked.

Dreary grinned, but shook his head.

"Never you mind, dear Quentin," Dreary said.

"You're compensated well for your . . . *companionship*, are you not?"

Dreary turned and looked the man in the eye then. Quentin had been riding with him for years now, plundering as he saw fit when Dreary would lead them from what had seemed one wild goose chase after another. But that hadn't mattered to Quentin. If the trail led to money or gold, he'd been welcome to it. If it led to guns and horses, he'd absconded with what he wanted. If it led to fresh, weeping widows, he had taken his fill.

They all had. Well, all but Bonham, that was. Bonham never took more than what he absolutely needed. Well, aside from lives, that was. He was Dreary's own personal angel of death. While Quentin and Avery had raped and plundered, Bonham seemed satisfied with no more than the opportunity to open veins and rend flesh. It seemed these were the only times Quentin ever saw the man's eyes come to life. When the big man wasn't shedding blood, they were as blank and cold as a pair of rocks beneath the surface of a steady stream. But when he was . . .

The man was downright scary. But none of this bothered Quentin so much as Dreary's mad quest. He'd stuck with the man for the plunder and tail, but he had become convinced the man was utterly out of his mind. Always pouring over that goddamned book with all the weird symbols and drawings in it. Always going on and on about the ancient ones, the elder gods, Egyptians and Injuns down south. Or tribesmen, or whatever the hell they were called. Savages with great structures Dreary claimed were built by and for these gods.

And then there was that one he always seemed to focus in on in particular. That goddamned N'yea'thuul. Quentin could hardly pronounce the damned word, though he'd heard it often enough in his years with Dreary. Some ancient entity lurking just outside their reality, waiting to be loosed back into this world to bring destruction, chaos, and ultimately, order.

Dreary was mad with search. They'd started way up north, near the top of the Chisolm Trail. Then they'd made their way south, searching out and then torturing and killing anyone with even the slightest amount of information. Always coming ever nearer and nearer to Dust.

They'd survived a lot. About halfway down the trail they'd heard tell of a massacre in the town of Duncan. Talk of some creature called a Wendigo killing cattle drivers and townsfolk alike. Dreary had seemed wary of this information. He was wary of anything that could potentially stop him from reaching his goal. His prize.

His destiny.

Quentin didn't put much stock in all of Dreary's ramblings so long as the gold and pussy was kept in constant supply, but here they were, right on the edge of the fabled town of Dust, the place they'd searched for all these years, through fights with Marshals and Sheriffs and Savages and narrowly missing a goddamned cannibal the townsfolk had called a Wendigo. Even managing to keep a step ahead of the gunslinger, James Dee, the man Dreary called The God Hunter.

Now they were at the finish line of Dreary's quest,

and his God Hunter was here as well, captured by the elusive townsfolk, and Quentin felt himself getting firm in his loins. He always enjoyed the quiet before the storm, when the blood would spill and the women would scream as he thrust himself into them. He especially liked it when their husbands would be forced to watch while Bonham and Avery held knives to their throats and Dreary demanded answers. He hoped he'd have a chance like that here. Today.

The first droplets of rain began to patter softly through the pines and he saw the red dirt of the street cough up plumes of dust into the air as the ground began to first absorb it, and then moisten, turning it to a thick, viscous mud. Quentin peered up, blinking the still sparse rain from his eyes as he beheld the darkening sky.

"Seems a storm's a comin', Gear," Quentin said, returning his gaze to the street. "Ain't nobody out. Where do we start?"

Dreary was peering through his telescope again, looking through alleyways toward the church at the other end of town with the strange coiling spiral on its steeple. He closed his scope and turned to Quentin and the others.

"If there's a Marshal or a Sheriff, we start there. And any deputies. From there, we make our way to the church."

Quentin and Avery pulled their revolvers from their holsters and cocked the hammers. Bonham pulled a large bowie knife from a sheath and seemed to admire the blade. That cold, dead look was in his eyes, but there was a flicker of something like a spark somewhere in the black of his pupils. It caused gooseflesh to sprout over Quentin's arms and all the way up his spine.

Dreary pulled a small Webley Bull Dog revolver—only slightly larger than his palm—from beneath his shoulder and winked to the rest of them.

"Time to take the spoils, gentlemen."

They crept out of the woods and down the mud caked streets of Dust.

14

THE LIGHT WAS better now than before, but it was still gloomy inside the church. Or temple, or whatever the skittering thing had called this place. Marlena could hear the rain pattering on the wooden roof, a constant beat of *rap-ah-tah-rap-ah-tah* that threatened to drive her mad. The skittering thing was gone now. At least she *thought* it was gone. After it had tied her to the large, black altar—if you could call it that—the thing had slinked back into the darkness and out of sight. That was more than an hour ago now, and she'd not heard it since. Nor anything else, for that matter.

Her arms ached and her mind reeled. What she had seen before, the wet, smacking blink of that terrible red eye coming out of the back of what seemed to have once been a man had utterly mortified her. The ragged wound where a head seemed to have been removed or perhaps burst now had a thatch of tentacle-like legs, mirrored out of the anus at the other end of the rotting corpse. The arms and legs of the man hung uselessly beneath as the skittering thing had moved about, swinging and lifeless as though stuffed with straw. But none of this had been the most terrifying part. What had nearly sent her into hysterics and threatened to tear at her sanity had been the mouth.

That horrible, unnatural mouth.

The side of the body the thing seemed to be using as a host was opened up from the armpit to the hip, straight through the ribcage. The jagged bones seemed to be some abomination of teeth as the ragged wound opened and closed while the thing spoke its hissing words, roiling organs and intestines within slurping and sliding around with every word.

She had been certain the thing would kill her then. Certain those terrible teeth or ribs or bones would tear at her flesh and the organs inside would slink out like a nightmare tongue and lap her blood like a dog at a puddle. But none of that had happened. With astonishing grace, the thing had bound her to the altar, the obsidian cube, and skittered away, leaving her for only God knew what.

Her binds were tight. She'd struggled for a time, but given up when all she'd managed to do was wear her wrists raw and bloody. Her thoughts were on Martin, her boy, somewhere here in all this mess. But they were also on her husband, taken by the very bad men. Only she still couldn't place his name. As damnable as that was, it was true. She could see his face, hear his voice, remember virtually everything else, but his damned name continued to elude her. The wound on her head had done quite a number.

It'll come to ya, Marlena, she thought as she tried to steady her thoughts. *It's in there just like all your other thoughts and memories. Those others came out, that'n will too.*

She hoped it would, anyway. She wanted to call out to him, to cry his name. Not that it would do any good. He'd been taken by the bad white men and was dead now for all she knew. But she wanted to call to him all the same. She just wanted to remember his name. It was a sweet name, she was sure of that. She didn't know how she could be so sure and still not remember it, but she knew it was true. And her head still ached and where was her son and *why couldn't she remember her husband's name?!*

Squelching footsteps somewhere outside caused her thoughts to seize in place. Even her breath caught in that moment as the slopping sounds grew louder and closer as someone or some*thing* drew closer to the doors of this unholy church. She squinted in the dark, her breaths coming in irregular hitches and she peered hard at the door.

When it swung open, the gray light outside, dim as it was, shocked her eyes and she was forced to look away, blinking rapidly. As her eyes adjusted, she looked back to the door and saw a blond woman dragging a young person in by the back of their collar. She threw the boy down hard and he coughed and wheezed as he struggled to his hands and knees.

"Get up there by your momma and stay put!" the woman spat in a harsh tone dripping with accent. "The Proprietor's on his way to see to the two of ya. If you're lucky, one of ya will get to join the Legion. Can't say which it'll be, though."

At this, the woman broke out in a cruel fit of laughter which caused tears to sting Marlena's eyes.

"Martin!" she cried, struggling fruitlessly with her binds. "Come here, baby!"

The woman was still cackling when Martin got to his feet and ran to his mother, clutching at her legs while she struggled fruitlessly to put a comforting hand on his shoulder.

The woman regained her composure and turned to leave. Before she got the doors shut, Marlena pleaded with her.

"Please, Miss," she said, tears now streaming her face. "Please let my boy go! I'm begging you, Miss, do you have children of your own?"

The woman's glare split into a malicious thing which might have been a distant cousin to a smile.

"I got lots of kids, lady," she said and spat to the side. "Least I did. They're all the children of N'yea'thuul now. Trust me, it's better that way."

Then she was slamming the doors shut and Marlena was screaming and calling out to her, begging her to let Martin go, to let him slip away through the woods, anything but leave them here with those terrible skittering things lurking about.

But her cries went unanswered, her pleas unheeded. In the end, all she could do was look down on her beloved son, peer into his beautiful brown eyes, and tell him how sorry she was.

"I wish daddy was here!" he said, tears soaking his own face as she looked at him through blurred eyes. "Daddy wouldn't let them do this!"

Marlena nodded pitifully, sobbing deeply, snot and tears pouring off her chin.

"I wish your daddy was here, too, baby boy."

She turned and looked out one of the side windows through a slit in the curtain which was drawn mostly across it. She could just make out what seemed to be an alleyway of some sort, the red dirt turned to a viscous muck in the ever-increasing rainfall outside. The familiar *suck-slop-suck* sound of feet sloshing through the mud came to her ears and see saw something which caused her sobs and breathing to cease at once.

Two white men with their hands up, another white man with a pair of guns on their backs, and a black man, also holding a revolver. A strange looking, *shiny* revolver.

But it wasn't the revolver that really drew her attention. It was the man holding it. He was familiar. Not just because they shared similar skin tones, but something much deeper than that. And all at once she was filled with joy and terror and galvanizing clarity as the last of her phantom memories came flooding back from the depths of her mind, spilling over the reservoir and flooding her thoughts.

"Denarius!" she cried.

Outside, the man's gaze shifted to the window and his eyes grew wide.

"DID YOU HEAR that?" Denarius asked, his voice choked.

James had. The men were leading them to the church, the place the Proprietor was supposed to be. Something about fresh meat for the Elder.

James pressed the barrel of his gun to the side of the asshole who'd had the revolver up on the ridge, the one called Roy.

"Who's in there?" he hissed into the man's ear. "What's the game here?"

Denarius had lost his focus. James saw the barrel of his gun wavering and dropping to his side. He didn't think the man called Mike would do anything. He didn't have the meanness in him like Roy.

"I asked you a question!" James said, growling now.

Roy's hands were up and James could feel the man trembling.

"I-I ain't on the scavenging crew," he stuttered. "Mike ain't neither! We just watch the town and keep things from getting out of control is all."

James pressed the barrel into the man's temple hard, the cold steel leaving an impression in the man's skin. Denarius was beginning to wander away, almost in a trance, toward the church.

"Stay with me, Denarius," James said in as even a tone as he could muster. Then to Roy, he said, "Start talking."

Roy gulped, shivering.

"Th-the the Elder is building an army. I-it all started w-with the Pr-Proprietor. He's the one found the marker. And it changed him. Made him like the Elder."

"Like N'yea'thuul?" James asked through gritted teeth.

"Y-yeah," Roy muttered, though unsurely. "Least I suppose so. Ain't no one never seen N'yea'thuul, just the Proprietor and his emissaries. We ain't got no choice here, mister! We can't leave or they'll kill us! Kill our families if we got 'em! Or worse, they'll turn us into one of those . . . those *things*. Oh, God, mister, even your nigger here should understand—"

James struck the man across the jaw with the butt of his revolver, hard. The man spat blood and teeth in triplicate, his face swelling, the lips split.

"I'm right sick of hearing that word," James said flatly. "I hear it again, I'll open your throat. Are we clear?"

Hate burned from Roy's eyes, but he nodded after taking a quick glance toward Denarius, who was still wandering toward the church.

"*Denarius!*" the faint shout came again from within the structure, and now Denarius halted.

"Th-that's my wife," he said, his face a rictus of confusion and horror. "I hid my wife and boy before they took me. Ain't no possible way they got found!

Why they here, Mr. James? Why my wife here? Where's my boy?"

Tears were collecting in the man's eyes when another voice, fresher and somehow more terrified came from within the church.

"Daddy!"

Denarius's face seemed to pale three shades as James was certain the man's guts were twisting into a knot within his belly. His eyes seemed to glaze before he turned, ghost-like, back to face the church.

"We're here, Denarius," James said to him. "We're here, and we'll get them out, now don't do anything rash!"

"They got my family, suh," Denarius said as though from a thousand miles away. "I can't just do *nothin'*. I gots to do something."

"And we will, just—"

Roy struggled to break free and James heard a *schlink* sound as a large knife came into view in the man's hand. It was coming around fast, glinting in the light and slicing through the rain. Roy's teeth were bared and a rising snarl was coming from the man like a volcanic eruption.

James had wanted to remain quiet. Wanted to use stealth to get into town and do what needed doing before breaking out the guns and finishing the town.

But there was no time now. No time to go for his own knife. No time to drop his guns and wrestle with the man. No time to use the force of his will to stop him.

All there was time for was a squeeze of the trigger.

Blood fountained from Roy's face as the man's lower jaw detached and spun through the air several times before splatting in the mud in a red shower. There was a deep, undulating cry coming from the man's opened face and his tongue lolled, slapping this way and that like a snake with a mind of its own. His eyes were wide and bulging as the cry rose in pitch and volume.

But he knife was still in his hand.

Roy stumbled forward, gouts of blood bubbling in sheets from his face, but he was raising the knife. One shot might not—*might* not—draw too much attention. But two certainly would. He couldn't risk it, not when they were this close and Denarius's family was somehow now in the mix.

James holstered his pistol and in a fluid motion drew his own blade from his back. Roy had his knife at the apex of reach, his high-pitched shriek an almost comical parody of a scream.

James brought his knife up and into the man's brain through the exposed roof of his mouth, pinning his whipping tongue in place as he did. All motor functions stopped at once and the man collapsed a second after his knife slipped from his slackening hands and splatted to the mud. James ripped his own knife free as the man was falling and wiped it on his pants before returning it to its sheath.

"Mike, you're going to get us into that church," James said to the trembling man. He got no response. "You hearing me?"

The man snapped out of his trance, looked away from the dead and jawless Roy, and blinked at James through the rain. Finally, he nodded.

"I ain't in any of this 'cause I wanna be, sir," he said. "I ain't got a choice."

James grabbed him by the back of the neck and pulled him close, bringing the barrel of his gun up under his chin.

"And I ain't giving you one, neither."

16

ENARIUS FOUND IT impossible to pull his jaw closed. His overarching feeling was one of stunned amazement, but there was a dreadful undercurrent of gut-wrenching horror beneath it that was threatening to bubble to the surface.

His wife. His *son*. They were here? But how? And why? Had they been taken by the same group which had taken him?

No, he knew better than that. Whatever was here, Mr. James had told him it was far worse than a pair of white hillbillies looking to sell off negro parts. Something more ancient and visceral. Something . . .

"Mr. James, I have to get in there," Denarius was saying from a thousand miles away. "I can't—"

"We're going, Denarius, just wait a moment, we ain't alone in this town and that shot's bound to have alerted someone."

But Denarius was walking on uneven legs toward the church, staggering this way and that. His mind was reeling. His head was swirling. He looked up and saw the steeple with the coiling spiral and thought madly, *what the hell is that?*

Then his ears were ringing and there was a sharp

pain in his left arm. His confused eyes darted around a moment, looking about aimlessly. Finally, they fell on the blooming rose-blossom on his upper bicep where blood was pouring from a small gash.

The ringing continued, but behind it, *beneath* it, he could hear shouting of some kind. He turned, in a state of shock and awe, and saw Mr. James with the fella Mike pulled tight to his chest, arm around the man's throat. James was against the side of the building in the alley and he was waving at Denarius with his pistol, up and down and up and down and—

"Get down!" he made out Mr. James's words as though they were coming to him from the bottom of a lake.

Denarius turned and looked up the street in front of the church and saw three men with guns, aimed in his direction. Their faces were snarls and their hands were thumbing hammers on their weapons and everything seemed to be moving through cold molasses and his wife and child were in the church somehow and *what the hell was happening?*

He was moving to his knees as the fancy gun of times yet to come was rising into the air in his hands as though in a dream. His knees splashed in the mud a second before he fired the weapon for the first time and knew in a whole new way what Mr. James had meant about the kick and the sound.

His hearing was utterly obliterated, only the faintest and highest-pitched hum rang in his ears now, and nothing whatever penetrated it. The gun bucked in his hand as though it had been hit with a mallet, the licking flame erupting from the end of the barrel let him know it was recoil from the monstrous round he'd just fired at the men in front of the church.

As he went down to his belly in the muck, his eyes fell on the glinting piece of metal on the breast of one of the men, the man who was even then twisting and grasping at his chest as a geyser of blood squirted under high pressure and arced into the air, chunks of red pulp whipping away into the air in front and behind the man. His face was a rictus of surprise and pain and horror and bewilderment. And the glinting metal on his chest continued to glimmer in the gray light and Denarius finally registered what it was as his hearing continued to be annihilated from the booming roar of Mr. James's Magnum.

It was a Sheriff's badge. Or a deputy's. Either way, he'd just shot a lawman in a strange town he'd never been before and probably shouldn't be in anyway. From the looks of the gaping and vomiting wound in the man's chest, he'd just succeeded in killing the man, even if the man wasn't quite yet aware of it.

"Oh, my Jesuuuuusss!" Denarius screamed as he splashed fully prone to the ground and he felt the wind of a half-dozen rounds zip over his head.

He began to roll toward the church, glancing up to see Mr. James throwing Mike to the ground in a wet splash before returning fire himself from behind the corner. One of his rounds ripped through the thigh of one of the remaining men. Denarius assumed them to be deputies, as well—as he saw them sporting metal badges on their breasts not unlike that of their fallen companion. Blood jetted from the man's leg and he went to a knee, but managed to stay upright, still firing. The man Denarius had shot was on his back and coughing a shower of blood into the raining sky, his movements slowing.

Denarius rolled under the church and took aim once more, about to fire, when a new sound finally penetrated his hearing.

"Don't move a goddamn muscle!" a man's voice growled.

Denarius turned to see two more men, these in the alleyway behind Mr. James. One of them, a large man with a thick beard, was holding a double-barrel shotgun to the back of James's head, baring his teeth through the thick thatch of fur on his face.

Denarius's jaw went slack again. The big bearded man too had a badge on his breast, but this one was larger and more prominent than the ones the other men bore. The man he'd shot must have been a deputy like the others.

This man was the Sheriff.

"Hell of a way to come into town, you two!" the Sheriff said in a growl. Without turning his head from James, he addressed Denarius. "That's right, black boy! I see you under the temple! Get your ass out here right quick and keep your goddamned hands where I can see them!

Denarius took several moments before crawling out, Mike's face looking at him frightened from the mud, but not unsympathetic, James's hard gaze telling him to do what these men said.

He rose to his feet next to the church, hands in the air, several weapons trained on him. From inside the church, he could hear the wailing cries of his family.

17

THEY WERE HAD for the moment, and James knew it. He could wait, bide his time, and strike when the moment was right, but it wasn't now and he knew it, not with a pair of twelve-gauge bores nestled at the base of his neck.

He lay his revolvers on a barrel at the corner of the building he'd been using for cover, not wanting them to fall into the mud and get muck in the mechanisms. Then his hands came up to either side of his head, cool as ice and not a tremble one in them. He could hear the cries from inside the church, could see the torment on Denarius's face, the tears which seemed to cut through the rain and make themselves known there.

He thought of Joanna, so far away from him and yet so terribly close in his heart. He'd come so far, through so many places and times and worlds. Was this it? A backwoods Sheriff getting the drop on him before he even got to the marker and dispatched the evil from the area?

No, his mind growled. *This isn't it. Not yet.*

James turned slowly, his hands high and steady, and faced the Sheriff. He was a large man, a face full of whiskers and burst capillaries high in his cheeks and nose. The scent of whiskey told James where the rosy spots had come from. The man liked to drink.

"The Proprietor ain't gonna be none too pleased with the likes of you coming into our town and shootin' up the place," the Sheriff said, an ever-present snarl around a few brown stumps which might have been the relics of teeth. "I do believe you've made one hell of a mistake, mister!"

James said nothing.

The Sheriff inched closer, his eyes narrowing in anger. James could sense Denarius being led into the alley by the other two men from the front of the church, one of them limping and gasping.

Good, he thought. *I hope it fucking hurts.*

"You picked the wrong town, mister," the Sheriff was going on, an insufferable monologue that no one was paying much attention to aside from the Sheriff himself. "If you only knew what—"

"Shut the fuck up, fat man," James said as flatly as he might tell a stranger good morning. "I'm here because I *know* what's here. And I come to send it back to Hell."

The Sheriff's features transformed into a rictus of surprise. Gone were the menacing, brown-stumped snarl and the narrowed, icy eyes. Now his eyes seemed too wide, his mouth circling into an *oh*. The barrels of the shotgun drew back an inch.

"The hell you—" the Sheriff began, but something behind him cut him off.

James saw it before any of the others. Though these men must have seen it before, perhaps many times, they all fell silent in a sort of reverent fear.

Denarius was the most shaken, however, as he'd never beheld anything of the sort, James reckoned. His jaw seemed more slack than before and his eyes so wide they threatened to pop out of his sockets and dangle comically about his cheeks.

"Silence," came a deep and inhuman voice layered in harmonies and octaves. *"Bring these two to the jail. The scout and the injured man will stay in the temple to guard the Elder's prize."*

It turned to the wide-eyed Sheriff. *"I believe you and this man have much to discuss. I want to know everything."*

The Sheriff looked back and forth between James and the thing, his gelatinous under chin wobbling beneath his whiskers.

"B-but, sir, he's—"

The thing held up a razor-tipped stalk or tentacle, silencing the Sheriff. The large, red eye above the two which had been those of its once human host blinked in the rain.

"I have spoken," the thing said, moving slowly through the muck, its human host's body floating as the dozen tentacles or stalks skittered through the mud, protruding from the corpse's back. The mouth was full of jagged shards of teeth and the chest was a razor-toothed cavity which dripped slime. The limp genitals quivered and shook as the thing moved closer and finally stopped five feet from them.

James saw Denarius's trembling form collapse to his knees and heard him say, "Jesus, Mary, and Joseph, what is it?"

His whisper was not acknowledged.

The thing leaned its host's body closer, the dead

eyes beneath the red one looking in opposite directions without a trace of life within them, the blinking, smacking red one above full of life, excitement, and malice.

"I am The Proprietor," the thing spoke through the ragged, open chest. *"N'yea'thuul will be pleased to have one such as you to savor. But first . . . "*

The thing brought a sharp tentacle to James's face and stroked it down his cheek. He could feel the skin split and warm blood begin to ooze onto his flesh.

"We must find out what you know."

The abomination began to laugh.

18

SEVEN YEARS. Seven *long* years. That was how long James had been here, from the time he stumbled into the town of Duncan on the Chisolm Trail until this moment. He was here. *Finally* here. In Dust. The place one of the Elders had its emissary building an army while it slept in banishment. The place it awaited its calling forth to bring the final destruction.

The place James Dee had come through the cosmos to end it.

But they'd gotten the drop on him. In all his travels through time and space, no one—no *thing*—had ever gotten the drop on him. It was his own fault, he reckoned. Allowing Denarius to come along had been what'd done it. He was fond of the man, had begun to bond with him. Allowed the icy edges of his heart to thaw ever so slightly. Had James not been concerned with the welfare of his new friend, he'd have likely made it into the church and destroyed the marker and then the town without issue. Only he *had* been concerned for Denarius. Denarius, whose wife and child had been taken unbeknownst to him and brought here of all places as food for the gods or as a host for its minions. The incalculable *odds* of the coincidence were staggering, though it *was* a coincidence, of that he was sure. There could have been no cause for anyone or anything in this town to have known he was coming, to have known he was so close. No way they could have known about his chance encounter with Denarius and the men who aimed to chop the man up and sell his parts for profit.

No. There was no way. No *possible* way. And yet, *all* of these things had conspired together, leading to James Dee, The God Hunter, being caught unawares and unprepared. Snuck up on from behind. Something which had *never* happened.

He wanted to slap Denarius. Hell, wanted to slip back to the moment he'd met the man and merely watch from afar as the sick men had done what they liked with him. To not intervene. The coldness he'd developed since his time in the void, after he'd banished the first *thing*—the one which had nearly killed him and his friends when they were kids and had come back twenty-six years later—was what had guided him through the universe and through time to the right places and had kept him on task, never wavering, never hesitating. Cold efficiency. Get in. Kill the gods. Move on. The rest be damned.

You have a pure heart . . . but you're not a good man. Perhaps you were once.

Perhaps. But what had Miss Dupree really known about him? More than he might have guessed, he'd gleaned that much from her, but she didn't know him. Didn't know what he'd faced, what demons had haunted him, both real and metaphorical. There was love in James Dee's heart. A great deal of it, actually.

Love for his daughter. For the woman who was the mother of his child. For his friend, the one he'd charged with watching over his child and her mother both in those final moments before he'd entered into the void and on to his mission which had spanned nearly two decades, seven of which were here searching out this damned elusive town. Yes, he'd been decent once, though plenty imperfect. It was the hunting which had destroyed that decency inside of him. The need for cold precision. When you hunted the gods, you didn't have time for friends. You didn't have time to do the decent thing. The greater good was at stake, and killing the gods could be the only goal. Secondary goals got in the way, got you killed.

He looked at Denarius again, not without pity.

Case in point, he thought.

The man's face was haggard and defeated. It was streaked with tears as they sat in the cell at the Sheriff's office while rain pattered away outside and ran through the roof in streams which were collected in a half-dozen metal pots about the building. Denarius was a good man. James had known it the instant he'd seen the man running through the woods, trying to get away from his pursuers. James had met a great plenty of decent folks in his travels since the void and what the Others had told him of the cosmos. Yet in no cases before had he deviated from his singular goal of finding and killing the gods of destruction to help a fellow person, be they human or some fantastic high creature from whatever world he'd been at the time. Not once had he helped. So why had he helped Denarius? Why had he risked everything after seven long years to help a man he'd never known?

DUST

You have a pure heart, but . . .

But. That was the problem. Her words had not left him since she'd spoken them to him. It was something he supposed he'd already known about himself, but had never taken the time to examine or dwell on. Since she'd spoken those words to him, he'd been able to think of little else.

Subconsciously, perhaps, he had been trying to prove her wrong. Prove to her and the world and to himself that she was wrong. He *was* a good man, both willing and able to do the right thing. Wasn't that the crux of his entire mission in life now? Doing the right thing? Sending these cursed gods into the oblivion beyond the void for good?

But he knew even as he thought these things that it wasn't enough. The world—the *universe*—was full of right things to do. Not just one thing. And he'd let himself become so singularly focused on the greater good, he'd forgotten all about the lesser good, the latter carrying as much dignity as the former.

"M-my family," Denarius was muttering to no one as weak sobs escaped his lips. "A man gots to protect his family . . . "

James leaned out, his thoughts of greater and lesser good, of pure hearts and decent souls swirling in his mind, and lay a hand on Denarius's knee. He gave it a squeeze and Denarius flinched, his eyes blinking and darting around a moment before falling on James, as though he'd forgotten he was there.

James nodded and smiled through his grimace.

"They're going to be okay," James said. "These men can't stop us. Just remember that and you follow my lead."

Denarius looked at him confused, his lips quivering and skin trembling. His head began to shake and his mouth opened on silent words.

"Trust, me, Denarius," James said, giving his knee another squeeze. "Do you trust me, my friend?"

Then clarity seemed to cut through the fog of Denarius's grief like a razor-sharp knife, and his eyes cleared. The trembling skin and quivering lips stilled, and the tears seemed to abate. He began to nod almost imperceptibly.

"Yes, suh, Mr. James," he said in a low croak. "I do indeed."

James nodded and tried out a smile of encouragement. He wasn't sure it was the right one, but Denarius seemed satisfied with it, and James leaned back against the wall of the cell and stared out at the Sheriff and his men, and the abomination called the Proprietor. They were all on the other side of the room, consorting amongst themselves quietly.

James could be patient. He'd learned it in all his years of travel and hunting the gods. You *had* to be patient to do what he did. All he had to do was wait for the right moment. These men, these creatures, none of them knew who he was. None of them knew all he was capable of. Of the magic he possessed. And what was more, he would have free reign of it here. He could slip through time and space with ease in this town, this *damned* town. Damned from its inception and because of the evil which permeated every square inch of its landscape.

Atrocities had been committed here. Were *still* being committed here. And while that was a bad thing, something that went against the pureness of

James Dee's heart, it was also a *good* thing. Evil made things *thin*. And for a bad man with a pure heart, that was oh, so very good.

James smiled.

19

MR. BONHAM CREPT through an empty building which may once have been a general store, but was now nothing more than a patinaed carcass in a dying town. He slinked past mostly empty shelves, past a forgotten sack of grain, its corner split open and the rotting remnants within little more than a pool of dust on the floor. A mostly empty barrel of oil stood near one window, its lip sitting several inches above the sill behind it.

Mr. Bonham smiled at this. Things always seemed to fall into place for him. It didn't much matter what the situation was. Once, when lawmen had been chasing him through a cornfield up north, he'd been in dire need of a weapon. Of something to fight the men off. A gun would have been nice, but he had no delusions of coming across one amongst the fallen husks. But he had needed *something*.

And while he had not found a gun amongst the husks, he *had* found the broken spoke of a carriage wheel, its tip nice and jaggedly sharp. Once that sharp tip had emerged from the lower spine of one of the lawmen—dripping great slops of black blood—he *did* get a gun. The rest had been easy.

DUST

Then there was the time he'd needed to quietly leave the Kansas town he'd been haunting for some time. And *haunting* was a more fitting word than most would realize. He'd been operating there for months, spying out winos and whores and the little sons and daughters of whores. Anyone he considered excrement. Mr. Bonham had no use for excrement, and he was not a live and let live kind of man. Not at all. Excrement was to be disposed of. If you saw it on your lawn or on the street, it needed to be cast out and away. If it got on your boot, it was to be wiped off.

No, excrement could not be allowed to perch on the streets. Not where he walked, anyway. He'd find them in the night, take them to his secluded place beneath the horse barn on the edge of town where he'd made his lair, and there he would dispose of them with patience and great pleasure, often shitting on the pile of body parts and slushy organs before hauling it all out to the pig pens a quarter of a mile out of town where all evidence of his work was devoured in four minutes flat.

Yet, the town Marshal had become a bit overly suspicious, so after feeding his bits to the pigs, he'd decided to get scarce before more lawmen came sniffing around. He'd made it only two miles out of town when once more, things had gone his way.

He'd met up with Dreary then, and not only had he found safe passage south with the man, he'd also found a nearly unfettered outlet for his bloodlust. Gear Dreary had little in the way of morals, and even less in the way of qualms against the appetites of others. Dreary was a man of singular focus, and their partnership had proven mutually beneficial through the years. And Bonham was a man who appreciated his benefits.

Mr. Bonham edged toward the window and unfastened the latch. With a gentle shove of two fingers, the twin panes swung outward gracefully, hardly moaning at all on their old hinges. He peered out into the rainy gray day across the street and to his left at the Sheriff's office. There was a big, beautiful window right in front, and within he could see several men discussing something together. Their demeanor seemed to say they were speaking in hushed tones, though he could hear nothing from this vantage down the street.

Then the door opened and some sort of abomination walked out. Mr. Bonham was not a religious man, but neither did he find the appearance of otherworldly creatures something to be awed by. They simply were. They existed. Rare, perhaps, but out there. They'd narrowly avoided a Wendigo—the reports alone had been enough to solidify his belief in the thing—some years back while still further north. He'd actually *seen* a Bigfoot once when he'd been far up in New England. Seen it and killed it before eating its heart and frying its backstrap into fine golden cutlets.

And now there was this . . . *thing*. He wasn't sure what you'd call it. Some cross between a man and a crab, or maybe a spider. But that wasn't quite right. It wasn't a *cross*, per se, but rather seemed as though the crab or spider were *inside* of a man's corpse and it was using him for sustenance. Like a parasite.

The thing had a giant, gaping wound in its chest with razor teeth which drooled and dripped, and a large, red eye burst forth in the center of its forehead. The spider legs which had torn loose from the flesh up and down either side of the corpse's spine kept the body afloat above the ground as it skittered away down the street.

Just before it turned out of sight, he saw yet *another* abomination join the first. This one was much like the other, but it seemed to have utilized the corpse in a much different way. The tentacles or legs came from the raw stump of the neck and right out the ass of this man, whose arms and legs dangled like limp genitalia beneath. The ribcage was torn open down the length of one side, the jagged bones like teeth, and the skin of the victim's back—which faced the sky—was bulged and split to reveal a blinking red eye much like the one on the forehead of the other thing.

Mr. Bonham, a man not unused to seeing strange and horrible things—nor averse to doing them— merely shrugged. He was sure it had something to do with Dreary's obsession, the *N'yea'thuul* thing he always spoke about from his book. Mr. Bonham didn't care. He'd learned enough about it from Dreary to know that whatever rite Dreary wanted to perform here would require blood, and that made things just fine with Mr. Bonham. Mr. Bonham liked blood. Liked the smell of it, the tacky feel of it on his fingers. The *taste* of it.

He nearly got an erection thinking about it.

He shook off the thoughts and focused on the moment. First things first. Take out any lawmen, and let the rest fall into place. They would move on to the abominations after. Those didn't seem to carry guns, but these lawmen across the way with their heads low in a circle and their darting eyes moving back and forth . . . they did. You took out the guns first, and the rest were easy pickings.

Mr. Bonham settled to one knee behind the barrel and rested his elbows across its top as he nestled the stock of the rifle into his shoulder. He aimed in the general direction of the window where the men were, then glanced up at the building directly across from him. Quentin was there on the roof, moving into position, aiming down to the side of the Sheriff's office. No one would escape through that alley. Bonham then leaned out the window just enough to see and glanced up at the building next to the one he occupied. There was Avery atop it, nodding that he was ready to roll.

Mr. Bonham's face twitched ever so slightly, the nearly unused laugh-lines on his face tracing his skin ever so shallowly before vanishing entirely. He nodded back to them both. He looked down the street in the opposite direction of the Sheriff's office and saw Dreary, hunched behind a trough, his Bull Dog in hand. He tipped his bowler's hat to Bonham and grinned in that deliciously vile way that made Bonham's heart race, for he knew when he saw it, it meant there would be blood. And a great deal of it.

Mr. Bonham turned back to the Sheriff's office and aimed down the sites of his repeater, took a deep breath, then let it out slowly.

He was salivating.

20

"**FIND OUT WHAT** he knows," The Proprietor said through the gaping, fanged wound in the chest of its host in a sort of whisper, "by any means necessary. Dig his testicles out with a spoon if you have to. The Elder will want to know how they found this place."

The Sheriff's face had gone pale at the order, but he gulped and cleared his throat, shaking off the thought.

"Y-yessir," he said, his voice a notch higher than he'd have liked. He cleared his throat again. "We'll get to the bottom of it."

"I don't need to remind you what will become of you and those you care for if you fail him," The Proprietor said in a low growl.

The abomination turned then and skittered out of the office on its spidery stalks, the sharp tips clacking against the boards on the floor as it went.

The Sheriff shuddered as he turned to his deputies, the only color on his face that of his beard, though it was mostly gray. The looks on the other men's faces mirrored what he expected his must look like, their eyes moist and wide, Adam's apples bobbing up and down on their throats as they struggled to maintain composure. None of them wanted to be here. None of them had wanted to stay after Reverend Sam Winston, the now dead corpse which The Proprietor inhabited, had discovered the cube and brought it into his church and had somehow unlocked the unholy horrors it held.

Elder N'yea'thuul sleeps, he had preached that day when the evil had come to Dust, eight years ago now. *And we are to prepare the way for when he awakens.*

The memories caused him to shudder anew, and he shook his shoulders animatedly in a poor attempt to disguise his discomfort. No, none of them had wanted to stay, but the things which had come out of that cube, that goddamned *thing* they worshipped and served, had made it impossible to leave. You served, or you died. It was that simple. At least it was that simple for a single man. Those with families were worse off. For them, you served or your *family* died. Slowly and badly. He'd seen what had happened to the former Sheriff's little boy, and being a husband and father, he had no desire to endure the same horror his predecessor had before The Proprietor had finally had mercy on the poor man and eviscerated him.

"Tommy," Sheriff Hollis said in a shaky voice, "you and Burt fetch some rope from back yonder. We got a job to do, you heard the ma . . . you heard him."

Tommy and Burt exchanged a glace before looking back to Hollis and issuing short, curt nods, the looks of men setting to work on something they wanted no part of but were powerless to distance themselves from.

Hollis gave his own, singular nod, not looking at them.

"Get to it."

They began moving to the back of the office, past the cell where the strange man and the black fella were situated, and into the closet. They began rummaging around as Hollis approached the cell and made wary eye-contact with the all too calm stranger. The man was staring back at him, not a trace of worry on his face. The Sheriff and his deputies had been speaking low, but surely the man had heard them. He *had* to. The office just wasn't that large, and there wasn't a stitch of rug anywhere in it to absorb even a modicum of sound.

The man gave him a smile. It wasn't malicious, defiant, or even scared in the slightest. The expression caused Hollis to pause in his approach, and he quickly reeled his chin back from his throat and clamped it shut, trying and failing to give off an intimidating demeanor.

"Calm down, Sheriff," the stranger said, his smile widening. "Things don't have to go so poorly for you. You got a choice here."

Hollis's wide eyes narrowed and he nearly blanched.

"How's that, stranger?"

The stranger laughed a soft chuckle as his shoulders rose and fell. The black man was looking at the stranger now with a species of confusion that simply had to be genuine.

"You and your boys over there," the stranger said and nodded to Tommy and Burt, "are in my way. I get the feeling none of y'all much care to be part of this, but you're stuck. I ain't sure just how, but that's my take on the situation. All the same, you're in my way. I'm coming outta this here cell in just a minute, and you can step aside and let me and my friend here go about our business, or you can die. Thing is, it don't matter much to me either way. I got no beef with none of y'all. But that *thing* that just walked outta here, him I got beef with. Him and his god."

So he *had* heard what they were saying. There was no doubt of it in Hollis's mind now. None whatever. He shook his head and gave his own version of an exasperated laugh.

"Mister, you must be thick in the head. You ain't got no idea what you done wandered into here. A man might think you'd get some sort of clue seeing our Proprietor here a moment ago, but you're too damn stupid to—"

"I know exactly what the hell I'm up against here," the stranger cut him off, all traces of smile gone now. "I come a long way over a lotta time to be in this place to put down just what walked outta here and all associated with it. It's *you* who don't know what you're up against."

The stranger was on his feet in an instant and he crossed the cell in two long strides, his hands clenching into fists around the bars of the cell. The explosion of movement caused Hollis to take a step back in spite of himself, and he quickly scrambled to regain his composure, his face etching in indignation and anger.

"Now, you listen here, mist—"

"You listen to *me!*" the stranger hissed. "I'm coming out of here in exactly thirty seconds, my friend and me. You can let us out, or I'm coming through, makes no difference to me. But if I have to come through on my own, I'm taking that as you picking a side. The *wrong* side. You get me, motherfucker?"

Hollis's eyes narrowed at the expression. He'd never heard it before. The black fella seemed likewise perplexed at the term.

"Mother-what?"

Tommy and Burt sidled up to the Sheriff then, Tommy holding the rope up.

"Got it, Sheriff," he said.

"Twenty seconds to go, Sheriff," the stranger said. The look in his eyes told Hollis the man meant to do precisely what he'd said he would, though he didn't know *how* the man planned to go about it. Still, a chill snaked up the Sheriff's spine at the determination in the man's eyes. Hollis's lips moved, but no words came. Tommy and Burt were looking between him and the men in the cell and back again, confused awe spreading on their faces like the look of a stupid cow seeing a new gate for the first time.

"I'd make a decision," the stranger said. "Fifteen seconds."

The black man , his eyes weepy but alert now, joined the stranger at the bars.

"I recommend you heed the man, Sheriff," the black man said in a deep baritone. "The things this man can do, I ain't never seen the like before."

The Sheriff glanced from one man to the other. He could feel his deputies next to him, fidgeting, waiting for orders. They were supposed to be tying the men up and dragging information out of them, but now everything seemed out of control. Not that he'd felt *in* control here in many years, not with The Proprietor and the other things skittering around town and sending out raiding parties for fresh meat and hosts, but this little situation had just turned itself on its ear, all thanks to this crazy stranger and his insane ravings.

"Tommy, fetch the ke—"

"Ten seconds!" the stranger roared. The man's knuckles had turned white on the bars and the air seemed to be shimmering around him, as though looking through waves of rising heat off a hot plain. And there was a sound, too. A weird, wavering sound, something like a . . . a . . .

A warble?

"You just hold your goddamn tongue, mister!" the Sheriff bellowed angrily, pointing his finger at the man. "I'm in charge 'round here!"

The stranger barked a laugh.

"*HA!* Five seconds!"

The Sheriff's pointing hand had begun to tremble and he lowered it slowly. The warbling sound was rising and the shimmering heat waves all around the man seemed to intensify. Hollis's lips were moving again, but like earlier, no sound emerged.

"Sheriff, what are we doing here?" Burt asked, his voice cracking, no doubt from the insanity they were all witnessing before them.

"Time's up!" the stranger growled as the warbling sound reached a crescendo and he and the black man were nearly obscured by the waving tendrils of air around them.

"Burt, grab the shot—" the Sheriff began, but stopped as two things happened at once.

DUST

Burt's head exploded as though a stick of dynamite had gone off inside of a watermelon, and the window behind them erupted into a thousand razor-sharp claws.

Tommy was screaming as the Sheriff hit the floor with a loud grunt and the air whooshed out of him. Gunfire began to erupt from the street outside, shards of glass and wood exploding and ripping through the air all around them. Tommy joined him on the floor, but it was a moment before Hollis saw the angry red wound on his deputy's forearm, spurting blood by the gallon.

"I'm hit, Sheriff!" Tommy was screaming like a pubescent girl. "Goddamn, I been shot!"

Hollis had time to see a blur of a man—*or was it two?*—snatching up the weapons from the desk before there was another nauseating shimmer in the air and the blur of the men was gone.

Then the door to the office exploded inward in shards.

PART IV:

A SHOOTOUT

21

THE FIRST SHOT from Bonham rang out sooner than Quentin had expected it to, and he jerked in surprise. The glass at the front of the Sheriff's office was tinkling to the boards beneath it somewhere behind the roar of Bonham's repeater, and Quentin jerked his gaze across the street, eyes wide, and stared in the open window to the dilapidated general store.

Blue ribbons of smoke billowed from the barrel of the rifle protruding from the window, and Quentin could just make out the dark figure of Bonham within jacking another round into the repeater with the lever, his movements masked in shadow.

"Son of a bitch, Bon—"

But Quentin's words were drowned out by the roar of the second shot. He heard wood splintering beneath him and leaned over the lip of the roof. Through a window below him, he could see a large man with a gray beard on the floor next to a corpse whose head was little more than a ragged stump of quivering meat. Quentin brought his revolver up and aimed at the fat man on the floor, cocking the hammer back.

As he squeezed off a round, a third man stepped into the frame of the window, and as the revolver bucked in Quentin's hand, he saw a splash of meat and blood erupt from the man's forearm through the scattering shards of glass.

Another scream as the man hit the floor. Gunshots were booming and popping all over the street now, and Quentin glanced up and saw Avery firing from his perch across the street from him. Blue smoke drifted in a thick cloud, hanging in the rain defiantly as the shots continued. Glass exploded and wood split into splinters in the Sheriff's office below. Quentin looked again to the window, raising his revolver to finish off the man he'd hit a moment before, but all he could see was the nearly headless corpse Bonham had dispatched.

"Goddammit!" he cursed as he scrambled to the corner of the roof for a better vantage.

As he leaned over with his gun before him, readying to fire on anything that moved, he saw something which caused his every motor function to lock in place in awed amazement. The wall to the side of the Sheriff's office, the one facing the alley above which Quentin was perched, was shimmering as though heat waves were rising through the soaking ground and through the pelting rain. Then two men stumbled through it and splashed into the mud.

And still, Quentin could not move. He couldn't react. He was faintly aware his eyes had tripled in diameter, and the scruff on his chin was tickling the top of his chest.

As the two men struggled frantically to their feet, recognition dawned on Quentin's face. It was the

James Dee fella and the black man he had picked up in the woods outside of town. They had somehow burst through the wall and—*and they had weapons.*

How in hell did they—

His thoughts were cut off as motor function returned to him all at once and a rush of adrenaline flooded his veins. He was swinging the revolver down at the fleeing men, thumbing back the hammer, readying to fire. Dee was in his sights and Quentin's face split into an unholy smile of triumph a second before reality seemed to tilt off its axis and throw him back into a state of stupefied awe.

A portion of the wall of the building directly behind the Sheriff's office further back in the alley took on that same shimmering, heat-wave effect. Through the eruptions of gunfire, he thought he could hear a strange warbling effect in the air, something unlike anything he'd ever heard before.

Once more, his eyes widened and his jaw loosened as he watched the two men vanish through the wall. A second later, the shimmering effect vanished, leaving only the weathered boards soaked in rain.

And there was no hole. They hadn't *burst* through the wall as he'd first deduced, but rather *slipped* through it, leaving it utterly intact.

"What the fuck?" he muttered to himself as he rose to his feet.

But there was no time to call his partners' attention to the miracle. As he spun back to the street, preparing to call out to them, he saw Avery jumping down from the balcony of a building and splashing into the mud as Bonham crossed the street in an easy, confident stride. The man slid the repeater over his shoulder and into a sheath, and a second later, in a fluid motion, he was casting the side of his coat out to reveal a dangling shotgun attached to a string within. The barrels had been sawn short, and Bonham fetched up the weapon in a practiced motion, thumbing back one of the two hammers as he did.

"Dee and the black fella!" Quentin began shouting absurdly, glancing once back down the now empty alley.

Bonham didn't even spare him a glance. What was he supposed to say, anyway? That they were ghosts? Specters who slipped through walls? And if that *were* the case, just how in hell were they supposed to put lead into something like that?

Quentin scrambled over the lip of the roof and onto the awning above the store he'd been perched on. His foot slipped and he slid off the end of the awning, managing to land face first in the mud. A second later, his head snapped up and he began spitting muck and dirty water from his mouth.

Avery was still firing into the Sheriff's office as Quentin saw Bonham mount the two steps up to the porch from the street, leveling the shotgun at the door from his waist.

It exploded inward in pieces no larger than a fist.

22

DENARIUS FELT AS though his stomach was going to come out of his mouth.

Not its contents. Nothing so normal as that. It wasn't like being sick after eating some undercooked pork or chicken, like the time Marlena had made him his favorite pot pie but hadn't let the meat cook quite long enough—likely due to the lack of firewood they'd had at the time—and he'd spent the evening in the outhouse expecting to see his toenails swimming at the top of the festering refuse beneath the hole their business was deposited. He actually felt his entire stomach sack would come up his throat, press its way over his tongue, and ooze out like a quivering, gray tumor onto the ground.

He'd seen Mr. Dee's power at work in the woods the other night. When he'd snatched the knife from his hand from more than ten feet away. When he'd opened a hole in the air itself and Denarius had seen into an alien world much like their own, though the trees and plant life had seemed foreign. But now, with blistering speed, Mr. James Dee had snatched him through not one, but *two* of those holes in the air, the first from the cell bars, the second through the wall itself a moment after snatching up their guns when the shooting had started.

Now they were splashing into the mud of the alley outside the Sheriff's office, Denarius coughing up mud now rather than his insides—*small mercies*—and they were scrambling down the alley, Mr. James dragging him along for the ride. His head was spinning, his stomach rolling, and there were so many damned shots being fired. He thought of the man in the office whose head had blown apart in stringy, chunky slops right as Mr. James had been conjuring whatever magic he possessed. He'd hardly been aware of any of them until just a moment before it all happened, his mind reeling with thoughts of Marlena and Martin trapped in this godforsaken town and he unable to get to them. But they were moving now, and fast. He could hear shattering glass and wood behind him, could hear screams coming from inside the office.

My dear God! he thought in a panicked rush as they neared the building behind the Sheriff's office. *Oh, my dear God!*

Then Mr. James threw his hand up before them as he veered them toward the outer wall of this new building. There was a shimmering effect Denarius recognized from what he'd been shown in the woods and the blurs of memory only seconds before when they'd scrambled from the office behind them.

And that strange sound.

They were through the wall and inside of what Denarius thought must have been a bank at one time in two blinks of the eye. He lost his footing in his disorientation and sent them both tumbling to the floor. Somewhere outside he heard the distant shout of man. It was a confused and bewildered string of words, as though the man were completely flabbergasted.

"That Dee fella and the black fella!" he heard the voice say.

But there was no more. Only the booms of gunfire and the screams of horror and death. He realized the shouting man had been referring to himself and Mr. James. Someone must have seen them. One of the shooters? Most likely. But who were they? Were they part of the Dreary gang Mr. James had told him about? He'd said he'd been tracking them, trying to beat them to this place, but they hadn't seen them at all and Mr. James had seemed confident they had safely made it and there was no way they could have found them here. *No one* could have found this place, except by sheer accident or precise knowledge of how to get to the path. Mr. James had been sure of that, and Denarius believed the man was absolutely correct. Had the men been following them? For how long?

Mr. James was shoving the Magnum from another generation into his hands and Denarius dismissed the thoughts as irrelevant. There were more pressing issues at hand than how the Dreary gang—if indeed that's who the shooters were—had found this place. They needed to get back to the church. Denarius had a family to rescue and Mr. James had a god to kill and a world to save.

"You alright, Denarius?" Mr. James asked him, bringing him out of his panicked fog.

Denarius blinked several times and gulped, his

throat clicking dryly despite being soaked by the pelting rain outside.

"I-I think so, Mr. James, suh," he said, trying to focus his eyes. "Is them the Dreary boys out there? I heard one of 'em say—"

"That Dee fella, yeah," James cut in, nodding. "I think so, Denarius. Fuck if I know how they got here, must have been tailing me. I'm a damn fool. I should have guessed he'd do something like this."

Mr. James shook his head, a look of self-contempt smearing his features.

"Doesn't matter now," he said. "They're here. We gotta deal with it. If we have an ounce of luck on our side, which I doubt, maybe the Sheriff and his deputy will get one or two of them for us. But I ain't holding my breath. I say we make for the church now, while we can make use of the distraction. The Proprietor is sure to have heard the commotion. Hell, the whole goddamn *town* probably heard it. Might give us just the time we need to get your family and stop N'yea'thuul."

Denarius was nodding absently again, savoring the reassuring feel the Magnum in his hand provided.

"I know I said I owed you, Mr. James," Denarius said in a shaky voice, "but I gots to get my family. They's all that matter now."

James met his eyes and placed a hand on his shoulder, gripping it firmly.

"You don't owe me a damned thing, Denarius," he said. "We'll get your family."

A thundering *boom* issued beyond the wall to the rear of the old bank, the sound of tinkering shards of wood following on the heels of its roar. There was a shrill scream, something Denarius might have expected from a young woman, even a little girl, but it carried in its tone the abject terror of a man who could see his end, was looking it right in the eye, and dignity was wholly absent.

Another thundering *boom* silenced the scream, and Denarius fancied he could actually hear the smattering slaps of blood and gore suddenly adorning the walls in the Sheriff's office, even from this distance.

"My dear, sweet Jesus," he muttered.

Then James was pulling him to his feet and dragging him to the front of the bank. He shoved Denarius to one side of the window near the front door and took up a position on the other. He peered out, his revolvers in hand, his steely eyes sharp and watchful. Denarius looked out as well and saw several people moving through the street. They were heading toward the sound of the gunfire, but slowly, as though moving against their will toward some unknown horror.

That was when he saw three abominations skitter into the streets as fast as scolded cats, spidery legs piercing the mud and limp, human appendages dangling freely beneath red eyes, two of the things with gaping wounds through their midsections, gnashing with bone teeth. One of the three, however, seemed to still have a living host. While the arms dangled, they were not quite so limp as the others. The figure inside the nest of horrifying legs and tentacles was that of a woman, naked as the day she was born, her face a rictus of agony. She wailed as the thing inside her carried them both toward the sounds of violence and death, her haunting voice carrying with it the chills of a soul trapped in a frozen hell.

"My, God, what are those things?" Denarius asked out loud, but not really directing the question to Mr. James.

He answered anyway. "Soldiers of N'yea'thuul," he said through gritted teeth. "They come through the marker from the depths of the universe, from *other* universes, and take over a human body. They eventually kill the person, but first they feed on their suffering and agony. Fear is food to them, and pain is a delicacy."

He looked Denarius in the eye. The look caused Denarius's breath to catch.

"That's what will become of the whole world if I fail here today. Pain, suffering, agony, *death*. The world over. Do you understand?"

Denarius gulped dryly again as he nodded, eyes wide. James returned his nod.

"Now, let's go get your family."

Another glance out the window showed the street had cleared of people and abominations. James gripped the door and swung it open and they stepped into the chilled, raining day. Gunfire continued behind them as they crossed through alleys and behind buildings, heading for the church. The sounds grew fainter as they moved.

Then a shrill, high-pitched roar that was neither human nor terrestrial punctuated all other sound and brought it to a stop.

Then, somewhere near the Sheriff's office, men began screaming.

23

REARY STALKED SLOWLY up the street, savoring the mingled scents of rain and cordite filling the air. It was an intoxicating mixture, made all the more so as the tang of copper whispered to his sense of smell as he neared the Sheriff's office. Avery was clambering to the street as Mr. Bonham stalked across, pulling free his shotgun. Above and to his right, Quentin was shouting something about Dee and the black man. Dreary had little use for the word used by damn near everyone in these parts in reference to their dark-skinned brethren. He didn't see them as mongrels or sub-humans like most of his pale-skinned compatriots. No, they were men just like he and everyone else. Their lot in this still new land had been a sour one, no doubt, about as poor a hand as had been dealt to any group throughout history. But neither did he see them as his equal.

Dreary saw no man as his equal. His intellect and knowledge of the cosmos and what sights it held hidden within were rivaled by no one. If he were being completely honest with himself—something he fancied himself to be rather astute at—*all* of humanity were subhuman when placed against the standard he posed. With their menial lives, working and toiling to put a mere pittance on the table for their families and themselves, most never seeing the world beyond a ten-mile radius of their homes, how could any of them compare with Mr. Gear Dreary?

Answer: they couldn't.

Dreary knew of gods and monsters, of fiends and ghouls, yet he was above them all. And soon, once he found the marker, he would make even the great Elders tremble before him.

Though he'd nearly dismissed Quentin's uncultured exclamation about Dee and the black man, his mind seized upon it now. Dee was *here*. He knew he'd made it to the town, and while he'd never heard the expected—and what would have been satisfying—gunshot marking the end of the gunslinger's troublesome life, he'd allowed himself to believe in his nemesis's demise.

Such a foolish assumption, he thought bitterly to himself as he glanced up the empty alley next to the Sheriff's office.

No sooner had he done this, than a muffled curse issued from Quentin above and he watched as the man comically splatted in the mud to his right. He allowed himself a small laugh as the man pushed up from the muck, spitting brown filth and water from his mouth while the rain patted on the man's hat, which had miraculously stayed atop his head in the fall.

The *boom* of the shotgun brought his attention back to the moment and he turned to see the door to the jail implode before Mr. Bonham into things which would serve well to pick food from betwixt sullied teeth. There was screaming from inside the jail, and Dreary watched with rapt attention as his steadfast companion, the insatiable Mr. Bonham, stalked through the gaping wound that used to be a door, leveling his gun before him.

Avery was coming up at his left, revolver in hand, and Quentin, covered in muck, had joined him at his right. Inside the jail, Dreary heard the muffled pleas of the fat man this town called a Sheriff as he held a hand out before him, begging for mercy. Dreary laughed again silently at this, the idea of a man begging Mr. Bonham for mercy. Mercy was an alien thing to Mr. Bonham. More alien than the rapturous creature that had left this building only moments before they'd opened fire on it. The man had a bloodlust in him that, had he not been one of Dreary's most trusted companions, might have chilled his very heart. But as it was, the man was his greatest weapon.

Dreary abhorred violence. He really did. It was not something he savored or relished. He did not wish it upon others the way some men did, the vindictive and the vile. But it *did* have its place, there was no doubt of that. While ugly, it served a purpose. It brought balance to an otherwise wildly uneven world. And most importantly, it cleared paths which might otherwise be impassable.

The fat Sheriff's hand vaporized a split-second before his jaw was torn free from above his jiggling throat. Only the smallest remnants of what had been the man's nose remained below wide and terrified eyes, one of which had been burst with one of the blast's pellets. Viscous blood and eye-pus oozed from the quivering man as his body tried to remain upright, not yet aware it had died. Then there was a fantastic spurt of blood from the man's mangled chest and his body fell over limp.

Mr. Bonham had not spared a moment in the exchange. As soon as the shotgun had released its final charge, he had broken it open, tossing the empty shells aside like refuse, and dropped a pair of fresh ones in its place. The metal *snicked* and *chinked* as he latched the action back in place and swung the weapon toward the other man in the jail. This man had gotten to his knees, his right hand clamped just below the elbow of his left arm, which hung askew at an unnatural angle, a red and angry wound dripping crimson.

"Just hold on a min—" the man began bellowing before a fresh explosion from the shotgun tore a hole the size of a cannon ball through the man's guts, sending yards of ropey intestines and shredded sacks of organs spilling to the floor behind him through the area where his obliterated spine used to reside.

The deputy's body had no pretense of holding itself up after it was dead like the Sheriff's had, and it folded up and crumpled to the floor before Mr. Bonham without ceremony.

Bonham turned, his gaze cold and emotionless, and strode back into the rainy street.

Quentin coughed beside Dreary, then spoke in haste.

"I-I seen that Dee fella, Gear!" he said, pointing down the alley next to the jail. "Him and that black guy! Went right through the goddamn wall!"

This didn't have the effect on Dreary that Quentin seemed to have expected as Dreary merely nodded to his less than bright companion.

"I expect you did, Quentin," Dreary said flatly. "Went into the building behind the jail here, did they?"

Quentin smacked his lips a couple of times, his eyes wet and wild, darting around aimlessly.

Finally, he said, "Y-yeah, Gear. Right through the damn wall!"

Dreary nodded and turned to Avery as Bonham approached them.

"Avery, you head around the other side of the jail here, Mr. Bonham and I will go this way. We'll catch them on the other side. We were fools for letting them pass on the ridge. We shan't make the same mistake twice. Once they're dead, we find the marker."

Nods issued all around, even from Quentin before the man realized he had no marching orders of his own.

"W-what about me, Gear?" he asked, the look of a stupid child his only feature.

Dreary turned to him and started to speak, even as Avery was making his way to the alley up the street from them, when a hissing shriek filled the air. They all turned and saw the abomination which had left the jail only minutes before come scrambling around the corner, followed closely by a similar nightmare. Gnashing bones of teeth clacked and snarled through the open wound of its mouth on the chest and the razor-tipped feet of its eight—*no, it was ten*—tentacle-like legs ripped through the muck, racing toward them with alarming speed.

Dreary ducked and ran for the alley Quentin had seen his nemesis escape down and took cover behind the corner. Quentin was close on his heels, pulling up behind Dreary. His face was a rictus of confusion and terror, the hairy flesh of his jowls quivering in the rain.

Only Bonham had stayed in place. The shotgun in his hand was cracked open once more, and he was tossing the spent shell aside and dropping another in its place as casually as a man picking at his food with a spoon. There was no alarm on his face, nor did he seem to be rushing against time. And time was certainly not on his side as the creatures scrambled toward them.

Dreary peered around, his Bull Dog in hand, and aimed at one of the creatures. The lead one with the mouth on its chest was nearest to Bonham, having passed a stupefied Avery a second before. But Dreary saw the second thing, the one with the mouth split down the ribcage, a moment before Avery did. He started to call out to him, but saw it would be a wasted effort.

Avery turned toward the thing only a half-second before the front two spiny legs—one protruding from the stump of the neck, the other from the anus of the host—thrust forward and through him with loud and revolting plunging sounds. Dreary could see the dripping tips of the thing's legs sticking out the back of Avery, one between his shoulder blades, the other directly above where the split of the man's buttocks was concealed beneath his britches. A wheezing scream issued from Avery, much louder than Dreary would have thought possible, as the thing lifted him into the air a full six feet.

In a fluid, ripping motion, the thing drew its legs apart with tremendous force and Avery's body was torn in two, his insides spilling in strings and splats to the muddy street. Yet the screaming continued, even as the thing whipped one leg, sending Avery's lower half crashing through window of a building across the street and Avery's upper half slid off the tip of the other with a wet slurp. He splatted to the mud, gathering the few ropes of his insides that were left to himself in a horror induced madness of self-preservation.

The screams continued.

Joining in the terrible chorus was Quentin, who Dreary glanced back to see was now tearing down the alley, the screams of horror and insanity tearing from his lungs in his flight.

"Coward!" Dreary bellowed after him, the word hissing out of him like a curse as it slithered from his snarling lips. *"I'll see you dead for this, Quentin! I cannot abide a coward!"*

But Quentin gave no heed to Dreary's warning declaration, instead continuing to flee through the muddy alleyway in a stumbling, terrified gallop.

Dreary—still snarling—looked back to the street to see the lead creature leaping into the air as Bonham snapped the shotgun closed, whipping it up to his shoulder, still as casual as a man on an evening stroll. The sound the thing made was monstrous and layered with unearthly harmonies of savage rage and hate, the snarling fangs of bone exposed beneath torn flesh, dripping with gore and anticipation.

It was fewer than three feet from the end of Bonham's twin barrels when both erupted with fire and pellets, the *boom* deafening to Dreary. With the ringing in his ears drowning all other sound, he watched as the creature was split from skull to groin down the middle of its body, the red eye bursting and spritzing into the rain as the body shredded and parted to either side of Bonham where its pieces slopped into the mud, slid a few feet, and came to an eternal rest.

Still, Bonham was unphased as he ejected the pair of spent shells and loaded two more, snapping the action shut. The second creature which had dispatched Avery in multiple directions was skittering toward them, and Dreary leaned out, aiming carefully with his small gun. The thing roared and reared up on its back four legs, six others spread out around and before it in a nightmare collage which reminded Dreary of some of the coiling spiral symbols in his book of the gods. But he did not dwell on this.

He fired a single round, which exploded the thing's single, red eye rising from the spine of its host, and the ribcage opened in a shrieking snarl of pain, one laced with the melodies of the distant cosmos. It began to skitter at first one way, then the other, not unlike a crab confused about which direction to go, then it began to spin in place, blind and furious and . . .

Was it scared?

Of course it was scared. It had crossed Gear Dreary on the wrong day, and now it would know a horror all its own.

Bonham glanced to Dreary and the two made eye-contact. Dreary nodded once to his calm companion, and Mr. Bonham stepped forward to the confused and terrified creature. He nuzzled the barrels of his weapon against the back of the thing's host, and fired.

Another fountain of gore erupted into the wet day,

splashing and mixing with the mud, and the thing fell motionless to the ground, only barely in a single piece. Bonham calmly set to work reloading his shotgun once more with a sniff as Avery continued screaming and wailing. More sounds came from up the street as men and women started to fill the street at the other end.

"Gear!" Avery began screaming and Dreary spared him a glance. His face was a rictus of pain and terror, blood bubbling from his lips and coloring his beard pink as the rain threatened to wash him clean. "Help me, Gear! I need help!"

Dreary almost laughed at this, but spared the man the embarrassment. No doubt his feeble mind was operating on fewer synapses than normal, and that was saying something. Instead, he gave the man a pitying look.

"My dear Avery, I'm afraid you're beyond help now."

Avery's face took on a puzzled quality, though the terror never left it. His eyes seemed to widen ever so slightly. Then he was screaming again as the murmurs and shouts of the townspeople up the street began to grow as they approached.

"Mr. Bonham," Dreary said as he shifted his gaze away from the people and the screaming Avery, "I believe we best be on our way."

Bonham nodded and joined Dreary as they hustled down the alley. As they went, the screams of Avery continued, and suddenly those of several of the townspeople joined his laments. There was a terrible shrieking roar, something akin to the sounds the abominations had made, and all other sound was ended at once.

As they slipped through the streets of Dust, Dreary thought he could hear the sounds eating behind them.

24

"WHAT IN THE blue hell is happening out there?" Jeremiah Quince asked, wincing as he cinched a length of torn cloth over the wound in his leg.

Mike was at the window, looking out through wide eyes perched over hard set lips. His stomach was in knots. Had been since he'd awoke that morning to go out with the other two scouts. As a matter of fact—if he was being perfectly honest—his stomach hadn't known rest in years. Not since the preacher had found the marker and unleashed hell on this already dying town. Since he'd been drafted into the service of the Elder by the thing which had taken over the preacher's body. The one they called The Proprietor.

Screams drifted in through the thin glass from across town. He couldn't be sure, but he thought it was most likely coming from the jail. Maybe The Proprietor was doing its work on the stranger from the ridge. Maybe Sheriff Hollis.

"Goddamnit, I asked you a question, Ennenbach!" Jeremiah hissed as he hobbled to his feet and began to limp toward him, pulling his revolver from its holster.

Mike pinched his eyes shut and hissed out a long breath. Jeremiah was one of the true followers of the Elder. A willing lapdog of The Proprietor. Not like Mike. Jeremiah didn't have a family with the threat of death and dismemberment hanging over their heads. Not like Mike and so many others did. The ones forced into servitude, guarding this damned town and its damned secret and its unholy temple. Jeremiah was taken with the power of it all. A free for all to act as he wished, so long as he didn't get in the way of the plan of N'yea'thuul.

Mike also didn't appreciate being referred to by his last name. It seemed somehow condescending, at least coming from such a man as this.

"I know about as much as you, Jeremiah," Mike said quietly, his eyes darting around, surveying the raining world of Dust outside. "Think I got a damn crystal ball?"

"Step aside," Jeremiah growled as he drew even with Mike and shoved him out of the way with his forearm, the barrel of his revolver clinking loudly on the glass.

Mike stumbled but caught his footing. He wanted to hit the man. He was rude, he was arrogant, and he was mean as a snake. It was this last part that kept Mike from putting his fist into the man's temple. The man was so goddamned *mean*. Once, Mike had been sent out with a scavenging party—something Mike was loath to partake in, but his family's lives depended upon his compliance—with Jeremiah and two other men. They had found a couple traveling by carriage, having come through Winnsborough not more than a day hence, on their way East. Jeremiah,

Mike, and the rest had stepped out onto the trail, blocking their path, and the man had pulled the reins on his horses, halting their progress.

Mike could remember the man's face then, concern etching deep lines through his face, his shoulders tense and rigid, his woman beside him, clutching to his side. They had been scared, and rightly so. Regardless of time or circumstance, a band of armed men stepping into the trail from the woods brandishing weapons was never a good thing. He supposed the man thought they were about to be robbed. If only they had been so lucky as to have encountered an actual band of bandits.

Oh . . . if only.

Jeremiah was the deputy, the rest of them like Mike—forced into servitude. The deputy had stood there for a long moment, and Mike had been certain the man was savoring the moment, drinking in the obvious fear on the couple's faces as though it were a fine bottle of spirits.

"W-we ain't lookin' for no trouble," the man had said, raising his hands as his wife seemed to be trying to fuse into her husband's side. "Just heading East is all. We have some foo—"

Without a word, Jeremiah had jerked his revolver free of its holster and put a round through one of the horses' skulls. Blood and brain and bone spewed as the confused animal—not yet aware of its death—bucked up on its haunches making a terrible whinny that still haunted Mike's nights to this day. The other horse had reacted similarly, but before it could take more than a couple of steps, its eyes wide and confused with the terror only an animal who knows no violence can experience, Jeremiah put a round through its head as well.

With the horses lying dead on the trail before the carriage, the couple could only stare in stupefied horror at the scene before them, clutching each other so tightly that Mike thought perhaps they might fuse into one being, after all. This had only seemed to throw fuel onto Jeremiah's blazing cruelty, as what followed had been the singular event that made Mike feel like a true coward. He'd served the Elder, done all The Proprietor had demanded of him up to that point, but with the soothing balm of telling himself he was protecting his family. He could have stopped Jeremiah that day. He knew he could have. *Should* have stopped him, he reminded himself daily, but had found he did not possess the fortitude to do so.

As he had watched Jeremiah pull the couple from the carriage, screaming and pleading, Mike had done nothing. As Jeremiah had blown the man's left knee off and kicked him repeatedly in the stomach, Mike had only watched. As he forced the woman to the ground, tearing her clothes from her writhing and screaming form until she was naked and soiled with earth, Mike had only cried. As Jeremiah violated her on the trail in front of her wailing husband, Mike had only listened.

He had been unable to watch.

The couple's end had been far worse, and Mike was reminded of it almost daily as he saw the soldiers still bearing their bodies, now rotted and shriveled, skittering through the streets of Dust.

Yet even now, Mike did nothing. Jeremiah was a mean man. A *cruel* man. And Mike was, quite simply, scared. In the years since the evil had been unearthed in this damned town, it seemed every ounce of manhood had been drained from Mike as his fear for his family had taken its toll on him to the point there was no atrocity he would not sit idly by and allow to happen.

And he hated himself for it.

"Sounds like it's coming from the jail," Jeremiah said, not seeming to address anyone in particular. "Goddamn mess! What the hell was that stranger trying to do, anyhow?"

Jeremiah's focus shifted from the gunfire and screams outside to Mike. Mike only shrugged.

"He was headed here, I told y'all that," Mike said. "Ain't seen the man before in my life."

Jeremiah stared at him for a long moment, then a smile which held no humor split his face softly.

"Hmm."

Jeremiah pushed away from the window then and hobbled up the center aisle toward the cube and the black woman—whom he'd earlier cut free from the binds shackling her—and her child huddled before it, weeping quietly on each other's shoulders.

"So that spook's your man, huh, lady?" Jeremiah asked the woman, as though asking a stranger where they'd bought their coat.

The woman looked up at him, her eyes puffy from tears but unable to hide the hate they held within. She didn't say anything.

"What's the matter, bitch? Cat got your tongue?"

Jeremiah started laughing quietly and hobbled a bit closer to them. He reached out with the revolver, the barrel now aiming at the back of the boy's head.

The woman's face seemed to recoil into fear, her lips peeling back over her teeth in a grimace of terror as she gathered her boy closer to herself, trying to put herself between the gun and her child. Jeremiah laughed again and tapped the boy's head with the barrel.

"How 'bout you, cub?" Jeremiah asked, his tone dripping with condescension. "That your daddy was out there? Huh? Think he was coming to rescue y'all, did ya?"

The boy only burrowed into the crook of his mother's shoulder and they both heaved with sobs. Mike watched as he had for years now—impotently. A tear stung his own eye as he saw the grief in the woman's face, knowing all too well how he would feel if the threats against his own family ever were to come to fruition. His hands were trembling, and the skin on his cheeks began to quiver as he felt a sudden and shocking rage well up inside of him.

"Jeremiah!" he said, trying to sound forceful and strong, betrayed by a small crack in his voice. He ignored it, hoping Jeremiah had missed it.

Jeremiah's back stiffened just a bit and he rose to his full height, still looking down at the woman and her child. After several agonizing seconds, he finally turned and faced Mike, his face set hard, eyes like ice.

He didn't say a word.

Mike's lips moved several times before any words came forth, his sudden rage shriveling back into him like balls from cold water. Jeremiah's look bored into him with heat and intensity. The man didn't like to be interrupted when he was having fun.

"The-these folks are set aside," Mike managed to

stammer, issuing a curt nod to punctuate the sentence. "They ain't fodder for anyone but—"

"I know who the fuck they're for," Jeremiah spat, vitriol lacing his words. "Think I'm a goddamn idiot, Ennenbach?"

Mike took a step backward even though they were twenty feet apart. He retraced his step back to where he had been with an effort.

"I'm just saying, is all," he said in a quieter voice. "We're supposed to watch them. The rest is up to The Proprietor."

Jeremiah glared at him for a long time. So long, Mike began to wonder if the scene had devolved into some sort of sick joke, one that wasn't funny in the slightest. He squirmed in place on his feet, uncomfortable and frightened, and was preparing to say something—*anything*—to break the terrible silence when Jeremiah began hobbling toward him down the aisle. When he was five feet away, he stopped, breathing hard and beaded with sweat. The wound in his leg was getting to him, but Mike knew the man was meaner than any gunshot.

"They're a sacrifice," Jeremiah said in a low tone, as though he didn't want the woman and her child to hear him. "Ain't nothing says I can't fuck with a sacrifice, so long as they're still breathing to be sacrificed when the time comes."

Mike felt ice slink down his spine and fill the crevice of his buttocks. Had he not been acutely aware of his swirling bowels, he might have evacuated all over himself then. As it was, he cinched every muscle in his gut and glutes and stumbled for one of the pews. He sat down hard on the wooden bench and sighed harshly. He was sweating too, now, and Jeremiah had noticed.

"Don't shit your britches, Ennenbach," Jeremiah said in a soft chuckle. "Now sit tight and keep an eye on the street. I'm gonna go blow a load in this bitch."

As Jeremiah turned from him and headed back up the aisle, Mike's horrified face met the woman's across the room. Jeremiah may have been talking low, but she'd heard every word. The abject terror on her face told him she had. And the boy was looking at him, too, he noticed. The look on his face was too much for Mike to bear.

He buried his face in his hands.

"I think I'm in the mood for some dark meat, bitch," Jeremiah said from the front of the sanctuary and began to cackle with laughter which echoed on the walls of the small church they had all come to know as The Temple of N'yea'thuul.

When the woman began to scream, hot tears spilled down Mike's face.

25

QUENTIN RAN.

His breathing came in wheezing heaves, punctuated by phlegmy coughs and curses as he weaved his way through the sloppy streets of Dust, the sounds of monsters and gunfire and dying men filling his ears, echoing off the dilapidated structures all around him.

He'd seen the abomination when it had gone into the jail, but his mind had simply not been prepared for the other thing, the thing *like* the first, but with the terrible mouth of bones and organs split down the side. He had not been prepared to see it tearing Avery apart with such speed, precision, and ease.

And oh, God . . . *the screams.*

Quentin thought perhaps the scream he heard now, the wet, gurgling cry assaulting his ears as he sprinted through the mud and rain, might be Avery's. He wasn't sure how it could be, the way he'd been torn apart, but the voice underneath the anguished wails was too familiar for him to dismiss, and it carried with it a haunting foreshadowing of doom.

This town was damned. Its residents were damned. It was infected with some form of evil too alien for his mind to reconcile and he feared the abominations were only the tip of the iceberg.

His mind, reeling as it was, managed to focus in on all the things Dreary had preached going on several years now. From his damned book. Quentin had dismissed these sermons as often as they'd arisen in his time with Dreary, casting them aside as the ravings of an obsessed madman. He hadn't cared about Dreary's singular purpose and drive. He only cared that he got to tag along and enjoy the spoils of his leader's warpath. The coins, the goods, the women. Quentin had been able to satisfy his basest urges in Dreary's company at whim, which was all that had ever mattered to him.

But now, seeing the awful truth of those mad homilies was tearing at the seams of his sanity. He could handle seeing a monster, but he could not handle the actual threat of one.

And of N'yea'thuul . . .

That was the true horror of his dawning realization. That his insane leader was indeed mad was evident, but his raving declarations were anything but. It was true. All of it. And if the abominations were any indication of what else lay ahead of him in this damned town, Quentin wanted no part of it.

He'd heard Dreary calling after him as his resolve had turned to so much toxic pus, oozing out of him in sheets as he sprinted away. Dreary was a tolerant man. But there were a handful of things he would not abide. Liars was one of them, but something he despised even more than a liar was a coward, and Quentin knew that if he didn't escape this dreadful place, the abominations would be only one of his worries. Dreary would come after him, maybe even sic Bonham on him. And Christ on his Throne, *that* thought was as terrifying as any of these otherworldly creatures.

He rounded a corner, wheezing and coughing in fits, and his feet fled from beneath him. There was a wet sloshing sound, and he found himself once more spitting mouthfuls of mud only a moment later. His entire front was covered in the slop, thick, sticky gobs of it clinging to his every surface. He whipped his hands, slinging chunks of moist clay free, and tried wiping them on his shirt. This did little more than smear the filth all over him, so he tried again on the seat of his britches with slightly better results.

Then he was on his feet again, running in little more than a stumbling trot, his chest heaving for breath and finding precious little. He had to get out. Had to flee. Had to—

He stopped short suddenly at the corner of a building, his eyes wide with caution and fear. He hugged his body up to the rotting wood of the structure and peered around slowly at what he'd seen.

Across the street stood an old church, its planks and columns split here and there, the windows tarnished and dusty within, rivers of rain sheeting the outside. The spire rose into the sky, a steeple of sorts, though the symbol at its top was nothing readily familiar. He squinted at it in confusion for a moment before blinding clarity burst through from the back of his mind.

The coiling spiral atop the steeple *was* familiar to him after all, only not something he recognized from other churches and places of worship. But he'd seen this before, and all at once he knew from where.

The book. *Dreary's* book, that damned tome he always referred to with the shit about tribes in South America and the words of the ones he called The Elders. The book he'd gotten all his ideas about N'yea'thuul and his obsession with joining what he called *the divine.*

The symbol on the steeple was identical to one he'd seen in that very book on numerous occasions as Dreary pontificated on the object of his obsession. It had been on a drawing of a black square or cube of some kind. Something Dreary had referred to as the marker. Right here, in this damned little town, was the symbol.

"Hell's bells," Quentin mumbled under his recovering breath.

Slopping sounds from his left caused him to shrink back into the cover of the alley, and they became louder with every passing second. He inched forward again, one eye peering around the corner, wide and feral. It was the stranger and that black fella. He *had* seen them vanish into the alley, no matter how crazy it had seemed, and here they were now, closing in on the church and armed to the goddamned teeth from the sight of them. The black fella had a shiny piece in his hand that looked nearly as alien to Quentin's eyes as the abominations, except for its similarity to his own revolver in most ways. But it was big, and he'd never seen a gun that shone so.

That wasn't important, however. What *was* important was that he was in a town full of creatures from Hell and a boss who would be seeking to have his head on a pike for deserting them in cowardice. And like manna from Heaven, right before him, the very thing his boss was after was right before Quentin, as well as Dreary's nemesis.

The vast lake beyond the church, which seemed to nearly surround the town on three sides rippled and waved in the rain. A scene he'd have found peaceful at another time, but which now added to his rising dread. Yet, the church, the *marker*, was right in front of him. Within his grasp. Getting his hands on it—or perhaps even better, on Dee himself—could set things right with Dreary. He couldn't hold Quentin's cowardice against him if he could convince Dreary he'd been after James Dee in the midst of the skirmish.

Abandoned you, fellas? Why, hell no, Dreary! I seen that snake Dee and the other guy getting away, I let out after 'em! See? See these dead fuckers here, Dreary? I got 'em!

It just might work. And having their corpses on the floor in the church with the marker would be all the better.

James and the black man halted for just a moment as a woman's scream filled the air, coming from inside the church, and another woman sprinted from around the side of the church, a shotgun in hand. James and the black man both drew down on her, but no one fired. Not yet. They were shouting at each other, but for the drumming rain and the horrible, nightmare roars of the abominations back across town, Quentin couldn't make out what they were saying. It didn't matter, though. Their words were of no consequence. What *was* of consequence stood right in front of the church, and the even greater prize within.

Quentin pulled his gun and smiled.

PART V:

FLASHPOINT

26

MR. BONHAM VANISHED around a corner and Dreary made to follow him. He could still hear the wailing roars of the abominations behind them, and because his hearing was focused on this, he jolted and slipped to the mud when the roar of Bonham's shotgun assaulted his senses and he was showered in sticky warmth.

He wiped at his soaking face and drew his hand back, registering the tacky blood there. He quickly began wiping his hand clean on his vest as he rose and saw another of the abominations collapsing to the ground in a wet slosh, its entire middle section a gaping wound which seemed to be wheezing some putrid, final breath as it crumpled.

"Good man, Mr. Bonham," Dreary said and patted his companion on the shoulder.

Bonham's head twitched the slightest bit at the touch, but aside from an affirming grunt, he said nothing as he tossed the spent shell and loaded a fresh one in his weapon.

More screams from behind them and the clamor of voices from townspeople got them moving again. They wasted no time. Dreary knew they were looking for a church or temple, something that would be marked with the sign of The Elders, the coiling spiral. It would be there he would find the key to his divinity. To become one with he who slept in the cold darkness of the cosmos, to awaken and draw that great sleeping god forth from the depths of the universe to wreak havoc and destruction on this damned world so that Dreary could rule over the ashes.

Despite his haste and apprehension, Dreary smiled as they ducked through one alley to the next, crossing the streets. Twice they encountered more of the abominations, no two of them precisely alike— some with still-living hosts, others dead and rotting—and in both instances Bonham dispatched them with hardly the twitch of an eye. The man was coldly efficient and would serve as a worthy general in the coming annihilation. Dreary could hardly have stumbled across a better servant had he searched the world over through eons of time. And once he achieved his divinity, perhaps he might just put that thought to the test.

So close, he thought to himself as they rounded onto a street and saw just what he was looking for. He didn't stop running, but his footing wavered a moment and he stumbled a bit as the dazzling spectacle sunk in before him.

It was a church. Nothing so spectacular as his dreams and visions had tried to conjure in all his years of searching, but it bore the symbol of The Elders at the top of its spire. Elation welled within him as copper flooded his mouth in anticipation.

I've found you! his mind celebrated. *I've found you at last!*

Bonham stopped short before him and Dreary almost crashed into the big man. He managed to get stopped before taking them both down into the mud, and he allowed Bonham's calloused hand to guide them both behind some old wooden boxes and barrels piled next to the building to their right.

"What is it, Mr. Bonham?" Dreary asked through hitching breaths, the rain running in streams off the brim of his bowler hat, his sodden bowtie a pitiful frown beneath his neck.

Bonham didn't speak, merely indicated with a nod of his head. Dreary followed the man's gaze to the front of the church where he saw Mr. James—fucking—Dee and his companion come to a halt before the building as a woman with a shotgun came rushing to meet them, her snarl evident despite the distance and the torrential downpour.

They were shouting something to each other, the three of them, but Dreary couldn't make out just what. There were screams coming from inside the church as well and the black man was becoming visibly alarmed.

The distance was too great to take any chances with the shotgun or their revolvers, but as though Bonham could read Dreary's thoughts, the man began tucking his shotgun on the string back into his overcoat, and then pulled the repeater from the sheath on his back. He lay the barrel over the end of a box in front of them and flipped up the rear sight. Bonham looked up to the sky for a moment, then back to the church. Seemed to judge something. The distance, maybe, Dreary guessed. Then Bonham began making adjustments to the sight on his weapon.

A moment later, the man was letting out a long breath and peering down the length of the repeater with one eye.

"Aim true, Mr. Bonham," Dreary whispered as he placed a hand on Bonhamn's shoulder. "The prize is within those walls."

Bonham grunted again and settled in for his shot. Somewhere behind them, the streets of Dust were growing louder with the sounds of approaching death.

27

THEY WERE NEARLY to the church, the screams inside no doubt those of Denarius's wife, when the snarling woman rushed around with the shotgun. James and Denarius both pulled up short, weapons drawn, aiming at the woman.

"You step aside, now, y'hear me, woman?" Denarius's trembling voice cracked through the rain. "I ain't here for nothing but my family!"

James glanced over at Denarius and saw the Magnum's barrel quivering in the air. The man's whole body was tense and James could imagine the inner turmoil he was going through. His wife's screams pierced the air like an arrow, the muffled grunts of a man inside beneath her tormented wails. He could hear someone else crying, a child perhaps, and knew this would only add to Denarius's crumbling self-control. He was at the edge of a breakdown, the tears clearly evident even against the rain.

The woman cocked a hammer on the shotgun, but she didn't raise it.

"Y'ain't coming in here!" she growled. "Them's in there's for The Proprietor and The Elder, now drop the guns!"

James nearly burst out with laughter at this. The gall of the woman, who'd foolishly rushed out on two armed men, not even bothering to raise her weapon. Did she expect one of the abominations to swoop in and take them out? James had no idea how many of the abominations there were in Dust, but at least most of them were behind them in town. Of course, it would only take one. Against an average man, anyway.

But James Dee was far from average.

"I'm giving you to the count of three, ma'am," James said, his voice silky smooth in contrast to Denarius's. "Then I'm gonna snatch that weapon out of your hands and put you down like a sick dog."

He said none of this with malice or any bravado for embellishment. He was merely stating a fact. As if he'd just told the woman it was raining out. Like it was obvious.

The woman's face cracked into a smile, revealing yellowed and browned stumps in her gums. Her sopping hair clung to her face like torn rags and her sodden dress had fused to her unglamorous figure.

"You gonna snatch my gun, huh?" she mocked him. "That'll be a helluva trick!"

She raised the barrel, but only about midway. It still wasn't pointed at them.

"One," James said as flat as a salt plain.

The woman began laughing in malicious cackles. Denarius took a trembling half-step forward.

"It don't have to be this way, miss," he said. "This man is full of magic. I seen it with my own eyes! Just step aside and let me get my fam—"

A fresh, sharp scream rolled to their ears from

within the church and Denarius jolted. James put a steadying hand on his forearm.

"Two," he said to the laughing woman.

"You sons of bitches come to the wrong goddamn town," she said as her laughter dropped off and her voice took on an ominous tone. "The Elder will not be denied, and The Proprietor will—"

"Madam," James said, cutting her off, "your Proprietor is in all likelihood slain as we speak. I've given you fair warning, and I aim to keep my word. When I count three, you'd best have that scatter gun on the ground and your ass moving away from it."

The woman's eyes widened in alarm just for a moment, but long enough for James to take notice. There was fear present in that brief instant, but the clouds of hate and malice rolled back in, obliterating all else.

"I'm gonna enjoy watching you—" she began, then stopped short.

James's free hand was out and the shotgun was flying through the rain—as though on a track—straight into it. It clapped in his hand with a wet smack. He quickly holstered his revolver and broke the shotgun open, inspecting the contents. Satisfied with the sight of two untouched blasting caps staring up at him, he snapped it back shut as he made his way toward her.

"Step aside!" Denarius was screaming at the woman beside him.

She did not step aside, but instead crumbled to her knees, her hands going up in surrender, her face a rictus of shock and amazement and fear. The fear was back in full force, all malice and hate scattered to the four winds.

James cocked the hammer of the shotgun.

Denarius shot a hand out as they stopped before the woman, about five feet away. He didn't touch James, only gestured for him to stop.

"She's unarmed, Mr. James," he said. "This ain't why we here. She can't do us no harm now."

James glowered at the woman before him, who now trembled to the point of quaking with terror, her wide eyes streaming tears and she begged for mercy through the repugnant stumps in her mouth.

"You ain't no man!" she was mumbling. "Ain't no man like I ever seen! Let me go! I beg you!"

"Mr. James, please," Denarius broke in once more. "You got business here, but it ain't her. And my family needs me. Don't do this. Think of what it means!"

James was already thinking of what it meant.

You have a pure heart . . . but you're not a good man.

"I'm not a good man, Denarius," James said without moving his cold stare from the groveling woman at the end of the barrels. "It's time you recognize that."

Denarius was shaking his head. "Yes you is, Mr. James! You a good man and you brung me here to get my family because they's good inside you!"

"No," James said in a near whisper. "I brought you here because this is where the marker is. Your family being in the same place is just a coincidence."

"I don't believe that!" Denarius shouted. His eyes were bold against his chocolate skin, full of righteousness and decency, all the things James had longed to be as a child. All the things he hoped to regain one day.

But today was not that day.

The shotgun bucked in James's hands as flames licked from its barrel and the woman turned into a crimson mist from the tops of her drooping breasts up. Gore spurted and coated them both, hot against the cool rain, and what was left of her collapsed to one side, the severed arms flopping beside her.

James looked to Denarius then, whose face was twisted into a look of horror and shock as he looked at the shredded remains of the mad woman.

"Y-you ain't had no cause . . . " Denarius whispered and trailed off. There was nothing more to be said.

James looked back to the door to the church and cocked the second hammer of the shotgun as he raised it to his shoulder.

"I told you I'm not a good man."

The door exploded.

28

MARLENA SCREAMED.

The man was standing over her, his filthy face peeled open over repugnant, blackened stumps inside his drooling mouth. His eyes were wild and ablaze with anticipation and lust—no doubt as much for her sex as for blood, Marlena reckoned—as she crawled backward on her buttocks. The man had his britches unbuttoned and was wrestling with the buttons on his long underwear. Grime clung to the exposed fabric of his undergarment, dirt and yellow and brown stains blooming in a sick parody of art.

Martin screamed then, causing Marlena to jerk her head to the right. She saw her son there, huddled at the foot of the stairs that rose from the sanctuary floor up to the hideous black cube that seemed to serve as a sort of altar in this godless house of worship. Marlena's eyes stung with fresh tears, not for herself, but for her boy, frightened and alone, though he was not ten feet from her.

"Mama!" he cried between sobs. "Mama, make him stop!"

If a human heart could have exploded under the weight of anguish for one's child, Marlena's might have then. She could feel it trying to crush in on itself, her son's confusion and fear like a mountain of lead bearing down on her very soul.

The man got his cock out. God, it seemed, had exercised brevity in His phallic allocation the day He had breathed life into the monster before her now, and for that, she supposed she should be thankful. There wasn't enough there to cause any significant damage to her, even fully erect as it was now. Still, it wasn't the man's mighty little mouse she was really worried about. His face was a twisted forest of malice, but his eyes betrayed the true depths of his depravity.

Whatever path this man had followed in his life, he'd found somewhere along the way an affinity for his basest desires. No, it wasn't just sex—that *dark meat*, as he'd said moments before—the man was after. It was power. Power over another, *control* over another life.

And he meant to take control now.

"Ain't had me a nigger bitch before!" the man howled as somewhere outside the distant sounds of gunfire and screams and the wailing shrieks of abominations drifted in through the thin walls. "Y'all's snatches big enough to take a real man's poker?"

Marlena had been continually scrambling away from the man, but as he spoke, her back and head struck something solid behind her and she could move away no further. Just as she'd reached the obstruction—a brief glance told her it was the obsidian cube—the man had spoken this last sentence. All her fear and terror of what was happening to her, to her *son*, all the adrenaline rushing through her veins and causing her very skin to ripple and sway, all of it seemed to take a moment's hiatus. The man's words, as cruel and disgusting as they were, had managed to strike her funny bone, and now they began to tickle. An absurd laugh belched from her throat, an uncontrollable thing, and it gasped past her lips. The man paused for a moment, three steps down from her, his twisted face of malice melting to one of confused astonishment.

Another laugh barked past her lips, more absurd than the first. Then another. They continued to slip past her throat and out her mouth, despite her mind's efforts to stop them. She couldn't stop them. Before her, even now, was a depraved and evil man, intending her perhaps the worst harm a man can inflict on a woman. But in spite of this, she couldn't stop laughing at him. Was he truly so ignorant as to believe the anatomy between races was actually different? And even if he was, was he so delusional as to believe that the pitiful little member choking in his hand—withering, she saw, even as she laughed—was capable of filling anything larger than an ant hole?

This thought brought fresh howls of laughter rolling up from deep in her belly. She was laughing so hard, in fact, that she actually grabbed her side as she slipped over to her left, propping on her elbow. The guffaws were deep, almost like screams, she realized. But they just kept coming, and no amount of willpower was going to stop them.

Through tears she could see the confused awe on the man's face transforming into quivering anger. His cheeks flushed red high on his face, his forehead turning to a nasty shade of purple. This almost sent her into a fresh fit of screaming laughter, and she looked away from him in an effort to keep it at bay. The whole thing was so absurd as to border on madness, but she liked this feeling more than she cared for the desperate fear that still lurked just beneath the surface of her laughter.

She caught a glimpse of the other man, the one who she'd seen with Denarius and the stranger. He'd been sitting in the pew, crying from what she could tell, but now he was staring at her, his hands still forming a cradle before his face. But he wasn't crying now. The look he gave was very similar to the confused astonishment the bad man had expressed when her mad laughing fit had begun.

Something struck the side of her face. Pain exploded through her head and her eye, and she tasted blood a second before she saw strings of it slinging to the floor from her lips. All the levity of the moment was gone in an instant, and the crushing weight of anguish and terror filled the vacuum expertly and instantaneously.

"You shut your fuckin' whore mouth, bitch!" the man growled. "You think this is a goddamn joke?"

She held her face with one hand as she pushed herself off her side and slid upright. The trembling was back and her breathing was coming in shallow gasps. She saw his penis again, flaccid and even smaller than before, peeking out from his underwear. But it wasn't funny this time. All the humor had been sucked out of the situation, horrifying sanity crushing it under the clarity of indifferent reality.

He was going to hurt her. Hurt her *bad*. She didn't think he would kill her, not intentionally, anyway.

She'd been brought here for a reason by one of those . . . *things*. No, other plans were in store for her. But it didn't mean something worse wasn't in store for her at the hands of this filthy piece of refuse. And God only knew what he intended for her boy.

"You gonna pull that black cunt out or am I gonna have to start diggin' for it?" he asked, his tone dripping with vile intent.

"P-please, suh," she started, swallowing hard in an effort to keep her voice steady, "not in front of my boy. *Please*. He's only a—"

Another slap across her face and her hands instinctively covered her belly.

That was when something clicked in her mind. She'd been struggling all morning since the knock on her head to get her mind straight. She couldn't even remember her husband's name for a time, so it was no wonder she'd forgotten this other thing. A fresh level of sickness seemed to ooze over her body at the realization and she looked down to the hands covering her stomach and the precious cargo within.

"Oh, my God . . . " she whispered as it all came back to her.

Denarius doesn't even know, she thought as her eyes glanced, fearful and wide, back at the man who was reaching out for her. *Oh, Jesus, Denarius doesn't even know yet!*

His hands grabbed the front of her dress, his fists filled with fabric, and he began hauling her toward him. Martin began screaming again. Marlena was faintly aware that she was screaming again, as well. Terror flooded every pore of her body and oozed out like a viscous gel, coating her entire being. As she struggled with the man, she caught a glimpse of his feral eyes, the dark stumps in his mouth, and his bobbing cock.

It wasn't flaccid anymore.

"No!" she screamed as he pulled her under him and began ripping at her dress, her undergarments, her thighs. *"No! No! NO!"*

There was a wet *thump*, and she felt it reverberate through the man's body and into hers. Her screaming had stopped. Martin's had stopped. The wheezing growls from the man on top of her had stopped. She looked at him then, his face settling back into a kissing cousin of the one from earlier which had displayed confused awe while she had laughed. But this one was slightly different. His eyes, for one thing. They were blinking rapidly, a tear caught in the corner of each. His mouth also was different. Where before it had been hung in slack-jawed wonder, now it formed a sort of *oh*. Drool began to collect near the bottom, preparing to spill over his lips, as one of his hands released its grip on her clothes and began to move toward the back of his head.

It never made it there.

There was another wet *thump*, this one underscored with a sickening crunch of bone, and the man's body jolted again. Then his eyes were rolling up in his head and he was slumping to the side. He hit the corner of the top stair hard with his temple and began rolling listlessly down to the floor below.

Marlena's eyes flitted several times, riveted in place on the man, then they looked up. The second man was standing there, breathing hard, his face a display of horror and confusion. In his hands, beneath white knuckles, was a large, bronze candle holder. Blood dripped from the thick base.

"Oh, my God," the man said quietly. "Oh, my God. Oh, shit!"

Marlena was already on the move. She got to her feet and snatched the candle holder from the man's hands. He didn't protest or fight her, but continued standing there, staring off into space, repeating the same words over and over again.

"Oh, my God . . . "

Marlena leaped down the stairs and, without thought, began to pummel the dying man's head with the weapon. The sounds were wet, sucking, sloshing, crunching. She wailed on. She wasn't aware that she'd been issuing a sort of growling scream until her son's voice finally cut through and caused her to stop, looking at him, her face speckled with blood.

"You got him, mama," he said in a soft voice. "You got the bad man."

She looked back at the candle holder in her hand, dripping with gore and blood, and she released her grip on it at once, sending it clanging to the floor beside the corpse. Her hands trembled as she stared at them while she turned in a slow circle. Martin came to her, and she embraced him as he buried his face in her stomach, crying softly.

A hand on her shoulder caused her to jump and turn with a scream. It was the second man. The one who had just saved her. His face was concerned and frightened, but there also seemed to have purpose there.

Her lips trembled.

"Th-thank you, suh," she whispered. It was all she could say.

He nodded, running a hand through greasy hair and putting his hat back on as he looked about the room.

"We, uh . . . " he began, seeming to search for words. "We gotta be getting you folks somewhere's safe. And I gotta get my family somewhere's safe t—"

There was an explosive *boom* just outside the door to the church. She realized she'd been hearing voices drifting through the door, but was only now registering their presence. She glanced to the door and then back at the man who'd saved her. His face was awash with alarm. Somewhere outside, the distant roar of an abomination bellowed in the streets.

"What's happening?" Marlena managed to ask in a tremulous tone.

The man blinked a few times, still staring at the door. She could hear more muffled voices outside. Finally, the man turned to her.

"Oh, shi—"

The door blew apart.

29

QUENTIN WAS SPRINTING through the street in a mad rush for the church when Dee blew the door open. His feet sucked and sloshed and splashed as he went, the rain pelting his skin like chilled needles.

Almost there! his mind howled crazily at him. *Dreary will be too pleased to kill me now!*

Dee was tossing the shotgun he'd snatched from the woman from much too far away, and while this trick of physics confounded Quentin, it paled in comparison to the abominations he'd seen skittering through town and ripping Avery apart.

Slosh-suck-slosh.

Dee snatched both his revolvers from his hips, thumbed back the hammers at either side of his shoulders as he started to march through the ragged cavity where the door had been a moment before, the black man stumbling slack-jawed and shocked behind him.

Slosh-suck-slosh-splat.

He was off the muddy street now, running across sodden grass. His feet threatened to slip from beneath him twice before he managed the proper footing, and soon he was barreling away again at full speed. His breathing was deep and harsh, snot bubbling from his nostrils and sucking back in with every heave. He was running up an incline, no more than thirty yards from the church now, and Dee was almost inside.

Just a little closer and I'll be in range, he thought, and pressed on.

Twenty yards. Fifteen. He knew he could drop to one knee and likely have a perfect shot. Neither Dee nor the black fella had noticed him coming yet, and for that he was thankful. What he'd seen the gunslinger do in the alley next to the jail and with taking the shotgun from the woman was *not* something he had any desire to face head on. A nice bullet through the back would do just fine and he wouldn't lose a second's sleep over it, either. Dreary would be satisfied and he could reap whatever spoils this damned little town had to offer as he would any other time.

A shot cracked through the air to his left, echoing through the sheets of rain twice before being swallowed by the wood and mud. He instinctively dropped to his knees and slid several feet, his arms windmilling about to maintain his balance. When finally he slid to a rest, his wide eyes took in a sight he almost couldn't believe.

Blood was spraying on the tattered frame of the door to the church and Dee was growling something incomprehensible, first thudding hard into the crimson-soaked frame, then stumbling beyond its threshold into the darker interior of the pagan temple. Quentin could now see an angry and spurting wound high on the gunslinger's shoulder, and the man's wide eyes were darting around, finally landing on Quentin.

Then, without grace or ceremony, Dee fell first to his knees, then to his face with an audible *thunk* inside the church.

Quentin's face was splitting into an awestruck smile that he wasn't even aware of when he looked back down the connecting street the shot had come from. Far down the lane he saw Dreary and Bonham stepping from behind a stack of boxes and barrels, the repeater in Bonham's hands still smoking in spite of the pelting rain cooling the hot iron. He started to raise his hand, to call out to them, when the wall of the building next to them blew apart as though a pair of dynamite sticks had just gone off. Wood and glass flew in all directions, and Dreary and Bonham were ducking and covering their heads, starting to turn toward the destruction. Dreary hit the mud and rolled away, while Bonham turned head on, raising the rifle.

One of the abominations came clambering through the destruction, tentacles and legs spread high and wide, a vicious, screaming roar issuing from the gory wound that served as its mouth. Even from this distance, Quentin could make out the angry red eye protruding from the skin of the poor bastard housing the awful thing. And . . . *was the person moving?*

Yes. Somehow, the host was still living, though in an apparent torment that seemed to echo the laments of the damned in Hell.

Bonham's repeater spit flames and boomed. The abomination twisted with the impact, a chunk of flesh tossed into the air, but on it came. One of its terrible legs seemed to have been wounded by the shot, as it seemed to skitter more lazily than the others. Bonham was sending another round home with the lever, resetting his aim. Dreary was to his feet now, and rushing toward the church, his tiny Bull Dog in hand. Another boom erupted from Bonham's repeater and crimson gel exploded from the terrible red eye of the abomination, a shriek accompanying it that froze Quentin's blood. The thing's spidery legs whipped in the air wildly as Bonham seemed to calmly load a fresh round into the chamber. Dreary was getting closer, not slowing at all.

The third shot seemed to end the thing's efforts, but not before one of the wild, thrashing legs hit Bonham across the chest and sent him sailing across the street, a spurt of blood visible for half a second before he splashed hard in the mud. Then the thing fell to one side and was still.

Quentin realized he was holding his breath, and a shuddering gasp escaped him as he resumed breathing. He was starting to get to his feet, one foot planted, about to rise to both, when three more abominations rounded the corner onto the street behind Dreary and beyond Bonham, a host of screaming people following behind them. Guns and pitchforks were visible, the rabbling voices little more than an angry drone.

Time to move! Quentin thought and stood to his feet.

The world flashed brightly for a moment and then Quentin had the sensation that he was spinning, not unlike a top. White-hot pain started to spread across his face and around the back of his skull as the white light began to dim scarlet.

He was aware that his face was submerged in a

muddy puddle, as he could feel the cool water over his face, his breaths bubbling from below. But he could see. It was a sickening feeling, this sight. It was as though he were on a ship, rocking in an angry sea, tossing at the verge of capsizing.

And through it all, he saw the black man slipping into the church, a smoking revolver in his hand.

30

"DENARIUS!" A WOMAN'S VOICE cried, and he instantly recognized it. He turned from the door, barely able to open his arms before both his wife and son were embracing him in tears. His throat seemed to close as he folded his arms around his family, and his eyes stung.

"Where are we, daddy?" Martin asked from somewhere near Denarius's spleen. "What is this place?"

"Shush, now," Denarius reassured his son. "Daddy's here. It's gonna be okay. Now, we have to help this ma—"

A man emerged from the shadows deeper in the church, moving slowly. Denarius tensed as he recognized the man, the same one they'd taken from the ridge when they first arrived in town. In a nervous motion, he swept his family behind him and raised Mr. James's Magnum. The barrel trembled before him.

"That's far enough!" he spat. "You just stay right there!"

"Denarius!" Marlena exclaimed, reaching from behind him and putting a hand on his forearm. "This man helped me. He *saved* me."

Denarius turned to her, confusion awash on his face. The man had done as Denarius had asked, and stood away from them, hands easily raised to either side. He said nothing.

"The other man, up there," Marlena said, moving her hand from his forearm to point toward the front of the sanctuary near the hulking, black altar. "He tried to . . . to . . . "

She couldn't finish. Her words became choked and her pointing hand returned to her and covered her mouth as tears spilled over her cheeks. It was only then he noticed the speckling of blood all over her face and clothes, the tears in her clothing.

Though she could not finish, Denarius didn't need her to. Realization crashed down on him and he was filled with grief and fury in equal doses. He looked past the man to the front and saw the dark outline of another man on the floor, the dim evidence of gore winking in the gloomy light.

The rain dancing on the roof was loud, creating an almost hypnotic drone in the large room. Denarius glanced from the dead man to the one standing before him with his arms raised. Denarius lowered the gun and nodded at him.

"I thank you for assisting my wife," he said as evenly as he could.

The man nodded back cautiously, slowly lowering his hands.

A groan from behind them snapped Denarius out of his near trance. He turned from his family and the man who'd saved them and saw Mr. James on the floor, a pool of blood collected around him. He was trying to raise himself from the floor, but was having little success.

"The marker," James moaned in a pained whisper. "Have to . . . before Dreary . . . "

Then his head collapsed back into the pool of blood and he lay still, save for the rise and fall of his back as he breathed.

"We gotta help this man," Denarius said, moving toward him and dropping to one knee. "He saved my life in the woods, and he helped me get to you both."

Marlena was at his side in an instant, tearing off a length of cloth from the bottom of her dress. Denarius rolled James over to get a better look at the wound.

It wasn't good, but it could have been worse. A couple of inches lower and to the right and it would have been through his lungs. As it was, it seemed to be no more than a nasty flesh wound. It could fester, he knew, but aside from a great deal of pain and some limited mobility in the arm for a time, he thought James would be fine. So long as infection didn't set in. The bullet seemed to have gone straight through.

Marlena tore off another piece of cloth, wadded it up, and pressed it into the exit wound. Then she began wrapping the first strip of cloth around his shoulder and cinched it tight, which James met with a wince. But the man wasn't conscious, either. His eyelids fluttered, showing only whites, then went still.

"That'll help staunch the bleeding," Marlena said. "But he needs a doctor."

Denarius nodded, looking about. He could hear rabbling voices in the street outside, getting louder. Could hear the snarls and bubbling clicks of the abominations as they charged. They didn't have time. No time at all. No time to deal with the marker, no time to stop Dreary, no time for anything.

"We've got to get out of here," Denarius said. "You!"

The quiet white man, still standing back from them, snapped his head in Denarius's direction.

"Check the street from the window and tell me what you see. I'll check out the front. Then we need to get this man and my family into the woods."

The man was nodding, his eyes wandering about the room.

"M-my wife and child," he mumbled. "Th-they're in town, as well."

Denarius stared hard at the man, not without compassion. But he was more worried about his family than this stranger's.

"Maybe we can regroup, get to them later," he said. "From the sound of things out there, we don't have any time. Now look out that window and tell me what you see."

The man nodded again, blinking rapidly and seeming to come out of a haze. Then he was moving toward the window.

"Stay close to your mother," Denarius said to Martin as he rose to his feet and headed for the door.

He stopped shy of the threshold and looked to the other man. He was stepping to the window, hands grabbing either side of the sill, eyes evidently wide, even in profile.

"How many?" Denarius hissed to the man after a painful moment of waiting with no response.

The man turned only his head to him, his face ashen and defeated.

"All of them, I think."

Glass exploded around the man, shards of razor-like debris burying into his skin causing a blossoming forest of wounds on his face and arms. A plum of crimson flowered from the back of his head then and a meaty pile of gruel spattered the floor behind him with a wet *smack* before he tumbled to the floor and moved no more.

"Jesus!" Denarius muttered and turned for the door to peak out.

No sooner had he turned, he noticed two things. First, the man he'd shot who'd been charging the church as he and James entered was no longer lying face down in the mud outside. And second, his belly was on fire.

He looked down, confused by the sight of spreading scarlet in his shirt and the handle of a knife protruding from his stomach, a mud-slimed hand gripping the hilt.

As he went down, he saw the horrific sight of a man, covered in mud and blood, one eye dangling from its socket. A second before his head hit the planks and he blacked out, he heard the man speak.

"Gotcha!"

31

SOMETHING BEGAN TO stir at the back of the room, something that no one still living inside the temple seemed to notice. The sounds of the abominations and the coming mob and the screams of Marlena and her boy drowned out the hum which began to swell from the black cube. Jeremiah's and Mike's blood on the floor began to slither like crimson snakes from the pools about their corpses toward the center of the sanctuary. Like living tendrils, then turned towards the marker.

The cube emitted a soft glow, revealing the designs of constellations and solar systems on its side, some of them things none of the others might have recognized, save perhaps the traveler, James Dee. At the center of the obsidian mass, one design glowed brighter than the others. A coiling spiral symbol, identical to the one atop the spire of the church, began to blaze brighter.

The blood from the men crawled up the stairs as gracefully as serpents, and upon reaching the marker, began to crawl up its side. The constellations began to glow brighter, the coiling spiral near the center brighter still. The hum grew louder, though still no one seemed to notice. There was an ear-shattering boom, a cataclysmic sound from out in the street, and the walls of the church shook as the windows on three sides all burst into tiny fragments, the pelting rain following in after them.

The explosive boom from outside seemed to have silenced those still living in the church, though the man with the dangling eye was still fast about his business on the floor with Denarius, his lips pulled back over his muddy teeth in a mad grimace of rage and desperation. Denarius was struggling on the floor with him as Marlena tried to stuff Martin between the pews, begging the terrified boy to stay hidden and still.

Then she was moving for the man atop her husband as the still unnoticed hum grew louder still, the glow of the cube's constellations—familiar and alien alike—began to intensify as the blood began to slurp into its surface as though being drunk.

She was almost to the man on top of her husband when yet another man—one she'd not seen before— rounded the door. He wore a bowler's hat and a bowtie above his vest and jacket, and his sopping beard dripped with rain. Marlena stopped short when she saw the man, and her scream was short-lived as the man raised a small revolver and fired at her. Her head whipped to one side then the other, slinging strings of blood lashing out like angry whips.

Then she collapsed to the floor, unconscious before James. He saw this, and wanted to raise up and blow his nemesis into the next century, but he didn't have the strength. He could hear the grunts and cries as Denarius wrestled with the other man.

Though no one had seemed to notice the sound of the marker, or the glowing solar systems on its surface, James had seen the whole thing from his stationary place on the floor, the pain and shock of his wound rendering him unmoving and thought dead by the others.

His eyes glanced up as Dreary stepped past him and into the aisle between the pews, facing the awakening marker. Though James could not see the man's face, he sensed its mask of wonder and lust.

"Mine eyes hath seen the glory," Dreary said as he took slow, steady steps toward the marker, the central glow intensifying still. "Behold the glory of The Elders! Behold the power of *N'yea'thuul!*"

Before James could muster the strength and resolve to get up, Dreary's form began to rise into the air before the obsidian marker, his body aglow with the light of the cube.

PART VI:

THE DIVINATION OF GEAR DREARY

32

ONHAM GRUNTED AND spat blood as he sat up. The abomination he'd dispatched was as unmoving as its host, whose terrible laments—which might have been sensual music to Bonham's ears had he not been locked in a life or death battle with the thing—had now ceased.

The clambering noise of a mob caught his attention and he turned to see three more abominations, followed by too many townspeople to count, all rushing down the street. There were guns and pitchforks and clubs in their hands, and the abominations snarled through ribcage and groin and spine, respectively, their bone teeth jagged and dripping ichor.

He knew there were too many to draw down on at once, even if he had more time and some high ground. As it was, he'd be properly fucked in less than a minute. He hated being properly fucked. He was a man who insisted on *giving* the proper fucks.

A glance back toward the church and he saw Dreary rushing away from him. This didn't anger him as it might have. Dreary was a man obsessed. A man with singular focus. Bonham knew from the day they'd begun to ride together that Dreary saw Bonham as nothing more than a means to an end. Bonham had never begrudged him that. In fact, he appreciated the upfront honesty of it. It let him know precisely where he stood, and what to expect of the man. And in return, he'd had ample opportunity to satiate his needs along the way.

A second before he looked away, there was the crack of a gunshot and he saw a man spin and fall to the mud in front of the church. Bonham smiled, recognizing Quentin's bulk, and he spat a wad of bloody spittle in his direction before turning away to face the oncoming horde.

Goddamn coward, he thought. *I'll join you in Hell directly.*

Dreary was mounting the rise to the church when Bonham turned back to the mob of monstrosities and madmen. He guessed there were a couple dozen men and women just behind the three abominations, and began to figure his odds as he reached inside the leather-lined pocket of his coat and curled his hands over the pair of cylinders he liked to refer to as 'his endgame'.

He'd had them for some time, tied together with twine and kept dry and safe on his person at all times. He supposed most men wouldn't want to have such a thing with them in a gunfight, but Bonham had never much thought about it. If he were ever to die, his aim was to take as many with him as he could manage.

And friends and neighbors, it was time for a grand farewell.

He pulled the two objects free from his pocket and swept them under his coat to keep them dry as he fumbled a box of matches from his shirt pocket. The box was moist, but not soaked. A small mercy.

He coughed a pint of blood as he knelt down in the center of the street, the horde less than thirty yards from him now and coming on fast. He got a match free, struck it, and it died nearly immediately in the rain. He curled over to block the downpour, seeing for the first time the horrific gash across his chest the dying abomination had managed to get in on him. He grunted dismissively at the sight. It didn't matter. Not now.

Another gunshot rang out behind him, much quieter than the previous ones. Dreary's Bull Dog. So, the man was at the church, charging on to his goal.

Best of luck to ya, Dreary, he thought as he pulled another match free and readied to strike it as the horde closed in to less than twenty yards. *I'll save ya a seat.*

This time, the match stayed lit as he moved it toward the pair of objects in his other hand. The fuse ignited and began to spark. Bonham smiled, blood-slimed teeth peeking out beneath his mustache.

He stood, coughing more blood, and tucked the lit dynamite under his coat to shield it from the rain. He looked to the oncoming horde, the wild faces, the abominable creatures.

He rushed them then, sprinting toward the crowd with a speed and agility most men in top form wouldn't be able to accomplish, never mind one mortally wounded. His lips peeled back in a vicious snarl, and a roar issued from deep within him so animal, so *primal* in its rage, the crowd before him seemed to slow. Even the creatures seemed to miss a step, their crimson eyes blinking in surprise.

But they were much too close to make any difference now. Bonham charged on, and surprise turned to outrage and madness upon all the faces in the mob as he began smashing into them, knocking down two of the town's people as he slipped between the legs of the abominations.

The snarling shrieks of the monstrosities rose in volume and pitch as the crowd of townspeople began raising guns and pitchforks and clubs at Bonham, but none of their voices topped the ferocious roar of the man.

The explosion was monumental. In all directions flew pieces of bodies—arms, legs, feet, hands, heads, torsos, and smaller bits. Quivering legs of the abominations whipped through the air, one impaling what might have been the sole survivor of the crowd near the back, and leaving the man in a permanent posture of supplication upon his knees. All screams and shrieks and roars were ended in the thundering boom, never to return again. Even the building where the earlier abomination had come crashing through was blown apart, and its columns and walls collapsed in on themselves, clattering quietly beneath the echoing of the mighty explosion.

Bonham neither heard nor saw any of this, though his still-snarling face—which looked chillingly like that of an insane smile—was etched onto his severed head as it came to rest in the street, overlooking the destruction.

A grand farewell it had been.

33

MARTIN WATCHED THE bad man who'd shot his mama walk past him in the aisle. The little boy trembled and shook, trying to hold his breath so the man wouldn't hear him. But he couldn't do it. His small body shook with fear and cold, a chill setting in from the rain, and he hugged himself tightly in an effort to control it.

But the man didn't seem to hear him nor notice him in any way as he passed, heading toward the weird black box at the front of the sanctuary. And Martin was only now noticing the glow in the room, one he was certain hadn't been there before. The gloom was dissipating with a soft blue light, one which seemed to be getting brighter.

He dropped to his hands and knees, still trembling, and crawled to the edge of the pew. He peeked around with one eye and saw the bad man— there were so many bad men these past days he was having a hard time keeping up with them all—slowly approaching the black box. There were strange shapes and symbols all over its surface, aglow with strange light, and a beam of that light seemed to be reaching out from the center, from a shape he recognized as identical to the one on top of the very building he was now in. The beam reached across the room, meeting the bad man, and seemed to envelop him.

The man began to rise from the floor.

Martin blinked several times, believing his eyes to be betraying him. But after a couple dozen flaps of his eyelids, he resigned himself to accept what he was seeing. The man was *floating*. Right in front of him, as if the beam of light were lifting him from the ground like the arm of some ghostly being. He'd heard plenty of ghost stories, mostly from his grandma who'd passed away last year. Neither of his parents much cared for the stories or his daddy's mama telling them to little Martin, but the boy had relished them. Only, in the stories his grandma used to tell him, the ghosts didn't grab you and lift you in the air. They walked in halls or graveyards, waiting to finish whatever was holding them back from moving on to glory or damnation, whatever awaited them beyond this world. And *none* of them ever reached out of a big black box in an old church that didn't seem to be a thing like the one he and his parents attended on Sunday mornings.

The man's body seemed to be tensing, his arms and legs arching behind him as his head lurched back. He could only see a portion of the side of the man's face, but he could make out the grimace there, whether of pain or shock, Martin didn't know. What he *did* know was that something bad was happening and his mother had been shot and his daddy was fighting *another* bad man with his eye hanging out of his face and the white man his daddy had come with was lying on the floor, either hurt badly or dead.

He didn't want to be here. He wanted to be at his house, eating biscuits and horsemeat with his parents and working the field. *Anywhere* but here. But the only way to get out of here was with his parents. He was scared. Scared for himself, for his mother, his father. He glanced to his mother and saw her chest rising, and a grateful shiver shook him.

She still living, he thought.

Then he saw his father and the other bad man, locked in mortal combat on the floor. Daddy was hurt bad, The bad man had stuck him with something, maybe a knife. He needed help, and the white man wasn't moving—

But his eyes is open!

Martin's gaze fell on the man, and they exchanged the briefest of looks before the man glanced past Martin once more to the floating man. Martin scrambled from the pew and rushed to the back of the church near his mother and father and the white man. His daddy howled in pain, grunting with effort. The man with the dangling eye was over him, pushing at the thing he'd stuck him with. His daddy was pushing the man's face away with one hand, trying to fight him off with the other.

Martin glanced around, his breathing coming much too fast, and looked for something. *Anything.* He needed a weapon. He had to help his daddy, and soon. There was no time to run and hide and though he very much wanted to, his daddy's words came to him, something he remembered his daddy oft repeating since he could remember.

You don't run from trouble, boy, his daddy's voice told him. *You face it head on, and deal with it like a man.*

He had to be a man now. His daddy's life depended on it. His mama's, too. If he didn't act—*and soon*—they were all dead.

Another glance about the room and his eyes fell on a candle holder, just like the one his mama had used on the man who tried to wrestle with her. There were several around the room and he rushed to one and snatched it up, knocking the wax candle it held to the floor with a quiet *thunk*.

Martin turned, gripping his new club, and rushed the man with the dangling eye.

34

THE DARKNESS BORDERED on absolute. The only visible light seemed to be tiny pinpricks, sparkling at what must have been a great distance, though they seemed near enough to pluck right out of the blackness all around. Dazzling, sparkling jewels floating in a vast nothingness.

And it was cold. *So* cold.

Pain was evident as well, as of something burrowing into the skin, then worming throughout the entire network of veins. Pulsing and dredging all the way to every extremity.

There was screaming.

The screaming at once seemed to be from a great distance away, but also felt as though it were erupting from inside, somewhere beneath the worms digging through the flesh, the tendrils of horrors unknown wriggling and writhing around the bones.

From the abyss in front, lost within a blackness impenetrable by any light from the twinkling gems which danced around, it came. Its shapes were all wrong, not in line with anything with which it could be associated. Angles that made the head ache for understanding, slithering monstrosities that must have been some sort of arms, yet there seemed to be dozens of them, and their movements were both staccato and fluid at once.

Further tearing at the edges of sanity were the words. For they were not words as man knew them to be. They weren't even foreign, like the tongues of men from the other side of the world. These were wholly *alien* to the ears, nightmarish sounds which assaulted the senses, yet seemed to come from *within* the mind rather than from without.

Blessedly—if one might call any part of this horror beyond all horrors blessed—there was a single feature which didn't send the mind tearing itself apart in madness in search of understanding and processing what it beheld. One thing on a being so large and vast, it vanished into the abyss behind it, seeming to have no end as it continued to emerge into the dim, twinkling lights of the sparkling jewels that danced in space.

It was the eye. That *horrible*, comprehensible eye.

This was *not* alien, not even foreign. It had the basic, commonly seen spherical shape of any normal eye. A massive black pupil hung suspended at its center, surrounded by a deep crimson where one might expect white. But at least it was a color a man could understand. Not like the shapes and tentacles and the rest of it.

Oh, GOD!

No, the horror of the thing seemed to be perfected in that one distinguishable feature, that horribly recognizable attribute. The *eye*. Gigantic, fitting for a beast of this seemingly immeasurable length and breadth. One might think there would be an audible smacking sound when the thing blinked—*and it was blinking*—but there was no sound. Only now was this anomaly recognized when the thing blinked. The total absence of all sound. A sort of vacuum which sucked that particular sense right out of a man.

But the other senses . . . oh, *God*, the others!

They were all frightfully present. The pain worsened as the thing continued to emerge from the inky blackness of what could only be the space outside of Earth. There was no other explanation. A place far, *far* beyond the peaks of the highest mountains, far beyond the white moon. A place of horrors and monsters.

A place of gods.

There was screaming once more, and now the absence of sound was made all the more apparent as the screams seemed so far away and so present at once. They were coming from within, but there was nothing to carry the sound beyond the lips to the ears of the monstrosity, if it had them at all. A smell of rot so strong as to be toxic seemed to fill the nostrils, though no real breathing was happening. Gasps of horror, silent in this place, went unheard and breaths seemed sucked from the lungs, expelled on silent screams as the eyes beheld that which they were never meant to behold.

The sounds came again. They had been present all along, the terrible, awful sounds that might have been words in another world entirely, but like the eyes beholding the sights before them, the ears were never meant to absorb these wretched mumblings, nor was the mind meant to try and make sense of them with letters and sounds it could appropriate. And that was when the realization came that the sounds were not at all coming in from the ears, though as the hands touched them they pulled away from the rivers of blood which flowed from them. The sounds were inside the *mind*. The *thing*, the monstrosity, the abominable damned thing *still* slithering from the abyss was inside the *mind!*

"Oh, God!" were the words attempted in a scream, but they never made it beyond the lips. *"What divine horror!"*

Sanity shredded entirely. Logic dissolved into vapor. Reason was utterly trampled. A cackling, silent laughter erupted then, shaking the agonized body, and multiple points to either side of the spine burst outward with horrific pain which was no longer dreaded but relished. The slithering feel of large stalks emerging from the burst wounds sending shivers up the spine, now coiled into a controlled knot from the cosmic beast.

"Ry'kuun N'yea'thuul Fhtean Ma'fhel!" the terrible sounds which were now wonderful, sensual things filled the mind.

And a sort of human understanding seemed to transcend as the coiling tendrils, the writhing worms of the great beyond, burrowed into the brain, bringing total understanding and utter madness into terrifying harmony.

Elder N'yea'thuul awakened comes!

The sight of the horrible, beautiful, ancient god emerging from an endless abyss vanished, as did the vast darkness and the sparkling gems within. The temple returned, the marker alight with the glow of the gods. The patter of rain on the roof and the spattering droplets through the glassless windows. It was all back.

Gear Dreary turned from the marker, hovering two feet off the ground on ten black—*and very sharp*—tentacles protruding from his back. The ache on his forehead was hot, and a touch caused something wet to seemingly bite at his hand. But he knew instantly with his new, unlimited knowledge, that it was no mouth, but an eye.

And without seeing it, he knew it was red.

He began laughing then, suspended in an agony beyond anything he could ever have imagined, but as sexual as the freest of brothel girls. The pain was pleasure, the agony divine.

He saw the gaping wound in his chest, the boney teeth snapping and snarling, the organs within lapping out like a terrible tongue. And still he laughed. It rose in pitch and volume as the mortals before him stirred and shrank.

This was godhood. *This* was divine.

"My dear Mr. James," Dreary managed to speak through the sexual agony, blood sliming down his chin with every word. *"The god-hunter has finally met his match!"*

The snarling laughter of the abomination that had been Gear Dreary echoed in this temple of madness.

"GEAR!" THE MAN over him growled in a maniacal drone. *"I got him, Gear! Ya see? I ain't took off on ya!"*

There was fear in that voice, a sort of tremulous testing of the waters. Whatever this man was doing, it was part of an effort to convince the other man—Mr. James Dee's nemesis, Gear Dreary—not to do him harm.

Denarius's hand was shoving at the side of the man's face. Wet, sticky slaps patted against his hand as he struggled with the madman, and through his blurring vision, his searing pain from the knife in his belly and the man's hands about his throat, Denarius saw it was the man's dangling eyeball that was smacking against his hand as it whipped around while they wrestled.

The realization sent a sick wave through his punctured guts. The nasty gash of a wound above the man's empty eye-socket informed Denarius that he had *indeed* hit the man when he'd fired at him minutes before, but rather than ending the man, he'd merely grazed him. Well, perhaps *merely* was too soft a modifier. A good quarter-inch sized trench had been dug across what used to be the man's eyebrow, and it had not only dislodged the eyeball, but rendered the socket itself incapable of holding it in ever again.

But he was a determined honky, Denarius had to give him that. The man's hands swatted at Denarius's as they struggled, and then the man had a palm on his face, shoving his head over to one side. Denarius could see Marlena there, a pool of blood collecting around her head. Panic and grief and horror flooded his already tantalized veins, and he cried out her name, though the word that came out sounded more like a garbled grunt than anything else.

To his surprise—no, his *astonishment*—Marlena's eyelids fluttered. Her head rocked ever so slightly, and she rolled off her belly and onto her side. Denarius was unmindful of the exertion he was utilizing against the man on top of him, the two locked in a sort of frozen dance to the death. He couldn't look away from Marlena with the weight of the man holding his head in place, but even if he could have moved, he'd have still been transfixed. His eyes were growing wider and a sort of dawning realization of shock, elation, and abject terror flooded him in equal doses.

As she rolled to her side, she pulled her knees up to her as her arms and hands hugged tightly to her belly, in an almost defensive, protective manner. Her eyes were still fluttering, moving about beneath the lids in frantic movements, but he caught something on her lips as she began to mumble something, coming out of whatever daze Dreary had put her into. He could see the seared flesh running down the side of her head, past her temple and vanishing near the back of her thick thatch of black hair, could see the blood oozing slowly from the grazing wound, and wanted to shout for joy that she was still alive and scream in fury for the injustice of it all.

But through it all, he focused on the wonderful, horrifying word on her lips.

"Baby . . ." she was barely croaking. "B-baby . . ."

Everything in Denarius turned to ice. The flame in his gut with the protruding knife was turned to a frozen lake as gooseflesh rippled his skin. He could feel the hot breath of the man atop him snarling into his ear as the pressure on the side of his head increased. Could hear the small, pattering footsteps of someone nearby, rushing toward him or away from him, he didn't know which.

And he could see Mr. James wasn't moving at all.

It's up to you, Denarius, he told himself. *Your life, your family's lives, and God knows maybe the rest of the world . . . it's all on you. Now get up and get it done!*

But he couldn't move. Try as he might, the man's weight on top of him was too much to move, no matter the frozen quality of the epic pain in his stomach. That hot, rancid breath in his ear again, the sticky, wet smack of the man's eye dragging across his temple.

"Just watch your bitch," the man was hissing into his ear. "Watch her while you fucking die!"

Denarius's eyes were blinking as fast as Marlena's now, his gaze still transfixed on her mumbling lips.

"Baby . . . baby . . . baby . . ."

Denarius began to scream then, a deep moan of anguish and fury and horror erupting from deep inside his perforated insides. His teeth were bared and his eyes went from spherical orbs of terror to ovals of black hate. Hate for the man on top of him, for this damned town, for Dreary, even for Mr. James, the decent man who was also a cold-hearted murderer. Regardless what had led him here, bad luck and the plight of a poor black man in this day and age, Denarius was here, and while Congress told him he was only three-fifths a man in the eyes of the law, all five of his fifths were a husband and a father and— *goddammit*—a *fucking* man! A human being who had a family to protect. He would not lie here and die in front of his wife and child, not without putting up one hell of a good fight.

All of his strength seemed to surge inside of him then, and with all he had, he began to push back against the man with his hands and face and every inch of his body. He didn't make much headway, not at first, but it was something. He was *moving*, and the son of a bitch on top of him was about to meet his reckoning.

"Just lie still, you nigg—" the snarling, dangling-eyed man had begun when a metallic *thunk* both silenced and rocked him.

The man began blinking, his face wincing in pain as the dangling eye swayed beneath the socket. And the force with which the man had been pressing down on Denarius eased all at once. Incredibly, both of his hands moved from Denarius and reached up, one snatching something in the air.

Denarius was moving, still encumbered with the man atop him, but no longer with the man's hands holding him down. He saw the man's hands wrapped around something that looked a bit like gold, but was probably bronze. The man's face was a snarling menace. His good eye a furious orb of hate.

And then Denarius saw the hand at the other end of the bronze object he now recognized as a candle holder.

Martin's face was beaded with sweat and his little boy was heaving breaths, terror etched on his features. He managed to let go of the candle holder a second before the man's other hand smashed into his mouth, a spritz of blood arcing into the air as his little head rocked back and he tumbled away.

The sight of his son being punched savagely in the mouth by the bastard on top of him sent Denarius into a fit of rage he'd never felt before nor thought himself capable of, and if this nightmare was ever ended, he hoped he'd never experience it again.

With a deep, snarling howl of rage and hate, both of Denarius's hands shot out and snatched the man's head on either side. The man hadn't been prepared for this, and the shocked expression on his face might have been comical had it not been associated with such savagery.

Hisses and grunts were all Denarius could manage as he sat up, grasping the man's head in his hands and ignoring the roar of pain in his stomach as the knife handle pressed against the other man, pushing the blade deeper into his stomach. But those pains were far away now, happening to another version of himself, the decent man who had vowed to help a man who'd saved his life, now dying on the floor, not of the father fighting with every last ounce of his life to save his family and do away with the slime before him.

The man's mouth began to form an *oh* as Denarius neared him, and his good eye widened beyond its standard limits. The empty socket next to it oozed and Denarius focused in on its dangling escapee.

His teeth bit down on the eyeball.

A sort of high-pitched screeching sound was coming from between Denarius's bared teeth as they bit down on the soft meat of the eye, fluids and gels bursting through its sides as it was pulverized between his molars. The man was screaming too, his rancid breath driving directly into Denarius's face. But he didn't care. He could only see red rage as he ground his teeth against the squashing eyeball and his incisors began to bite the cords in two.

Blood sprayed as Denarius ripped his head backward in a savage arc, his screech turning to a growl. The other man had lost all focus except that which was on his ruined eye. His hands went to his face as he tumbled back off of Denarius and onto the floor. But Denarius didn't stop coming. He scrambled on top of the man, his teeth still bared and ocular fluids dripping from between his teeth as he leaned over the top of the man, snarling.

The man was starting to notice him, but only just. He was still howling and holding his face, but his remaining eye was coming around to focus on Denarius, hate and fear present in equal measures.

Denarius ripped the knife out of his own gut, hardly noticing the horrific symphony of pain that shot through his entire body when he did. Then the knife was over his head and his free hand was clamped over the man's throat. He leaned in closer and spat the pulverized remains of the man's eye onto his face in a gelatinous heap. It looked like a half-chewed grape, but the color was all wrong.

"Mothafucka touch my kid, that mothafucka dies!" Denarius howled in wild fury, using the foreign term he'd heard Mr. James use back at the jail.

No term ever seemed so fitting.

The man seemed to have been sucking air in to talk or to scream some more when the blade buried into his chest. There was a wheezing whistle as air escaped his lungs around the hilt pressing against his chest. A moment later, blood erupted like crimson lava from his mouth, dripping down the sides of his face and onto the floor, as well as into the empty socket of his eye. Gurgles were the extent of the sounds the man made as Denarius ripped the blade out and drove it back into the man repeatedly with a maddened vigor. Blood slung about in ropes and strings as he worked, not slowing until the pain in his gut and the darkening at the edges of his vision brought him back to the reality of his badly wounded state.

As Martin was getting to his feet, nursing his split lip in his hand, Denarius drove the knife through the front of the man's throat, severing the Adam's Apple, and left the blade there. He tried to reach for his son as he approached, but fell to his side.

Marlena was there, still woozy from the looks of her, but coming around. She was putting an arm beneath Denarius's head, cradling him in her lap while Martin hugged his daddy tightly about the chest, causing Denarius to wince in pain. Martin pulled back and looked down at his father's wounded stomach and began to cry.

"Daddy?" the boy blubbered and stopped. He could say no more.

Denarius put a hand on his shoulder and squeezed.

"Gonna be alright, Martin," he whispered, tasting copper on his tongue. "We gonna be al—"

That was when they all heard the cackling laughter of the man in the aisle before the glowing black cube. The man with spider-like legs coming out of his back and a gaping wound of a mouth smacking and dripping at the center of his chest. The man with a huge red eye blinking wetly from his forehead, just beneath his upturned bowler's hat.

They all began screaming.

PART VII:

AWAKENING

36

THE SKITTERING STEPS of the Dreary-thing clicked across the wooden planks of the floor, a wet, bubbling sound which seemed to click rapidly rumbled from the horror of its chest. Dreary's eyes were rolled back and fluttering, coming back into focus for a moment, then out again. His face writhed in agony, yet he still managed a sort of maniacal laughter, quiet and utterly mad, issuing from his blood-slimed mouth. His beard was caked in crimson.

It was almost as if Dreary weren't there at all, at least not in the forefront. Like he was some sort of walk-on player in the background of a stage as the real action played out at the front with the real stars of the show.

But the red eye did not flutter. It was focused and hungry with want. The abominable thing blinked every so often, and James could hear it in spite of the gurgling and the bubbling and the clicking and the *tick-a-tick-a-tick-a* of its skittering steps on its alien stalks across the floor. The mouth on its chest snapped shut and open again, the bones almost chiming as they brushed each other, the organs within actually *moving* about as if they were independent beings themselves.

James was struggling to his hands and knees, his wounded left shoulder dripping blood, the arm attached curled against his chest. He winced, tears stinging his eyes as he rose defiantly before the beast.

The Dreary-thing stopped several feet away from him, the screams of Denarius and his family subsiding into fevered gasps of horror behind him. James could *feel* them trembling. While every part of his being was intent on ending the creature and destroying the marker at any cost whatever, something deep in his subconscious felt the need to protect these people. It wasn't exactly something *new,* this feeling, but in all his time of hunting down gods and their soldiers throughout the years and the cosmos, he'd grown a thick and almost impenetrable callous around his heart, like a cocoon, not letting decency or goodness or the right thing interfere with his mission. He'd sacrificed countless beings throughout many worlds in his quest to bring down the elder gods, yet something about this man and his family had managed to prick his heart through the thick covering he'd woven it within. Perhaps it was the inherent goodness of this man, his determination to repay the good deed to James for having saved his life. Perhaps it was the troubling words of Miss Dupree, observing his purity of heart as well as the sacrifice of his own goodness. He had been a good man once. A troubled one, to be sure, but a decent man at heart. He thought to his childhood, playing with his friends in the woods, not all that far from here, but many years away from where he was now. Remembered facing down his first monster in that damned place in the woods, what he and his friends had done, not only to survive, but also to save the world. Had that been the beginning of what would finally eat away the goodness within him? He thought so. The decisions he'd made—that he and *all* of his friends had made—had led to a life of drink and sorrow and nightmares. Had led to the conception of his beautiful daughter Joanna, and the sacrifice he'd made twenty-six years later when they'd faced the monster a second time. Had he damned himself then, as a child? Had he redeemed himself as an adult? He liked to think so, but in the years since then, since his time in the void with The Others, he'd murdered his way across the galaxies, letting nothing stand in his way or in that of his mission, killing the gods, the demi-gods, and the monsters infecting reality.

He got to his feet shakily, wincing at the pain in his arm, and shuddered. He felt weak, lightheaded. But if there were any shred of decency left in him, any glowing ember of goodness remaining, he knew now it was imperative that he not let it be quenched. It had to be protected, fostered, and allowed to bloom into flame once more. Not only did his soul depend upon it, but also the lives of the good people in this damnable place with him.

He rose to his full height, the Dreary-thing leering at him with its repulsive red eye. James grimaced, taking a single, uneven step toward the thing.

"It's over, Dreary," he said, addressing the thing by its host's name, though he knew he wasn't really speaking to Dreary. "The town isn't yours anymore. It isn't N'yea'thuul's anymore. You're beaten."

The angry wound on the Dreary-thing's chest began to gnash open and shut with gurgling laughter.

Dreary's eyes focused again for a moment, a look of absolute horror in them, then they fluttered again and rolled up, exposing the whites.

The red eye blinked with malice.

"You're wrong, god-hunter," the thing said through the dripping chest of its host. *"N'yea'thuul is awakened, and he comes. His army will be rebuilt, in numbers you cannot even fathom in your pitiful human mind. Soon, this world will be his playground, and when he has finished wiping every last shred of life from this puny planet, well . . . "*

The Dreary-thing trailed off with a chuckle of laughter.

"Well, then . . . there's a whole universe of worlds to devour."

James's face was set hard, his lips a flat line.

"That's where you're wrong, Dreary," he said, shaking his head. "You only thought you were joining the divine. Instead it has devoured you. And if N'yea'thuul wants this world, he's going to have to come through me to get it."

The Dreary-thing cackled a repugnant belch of laughter.

"You, god-hunter?" it asked, amused. *"You may have been lucky with the other gods, but you are no match for N'yea'thuul!"*

Two of the thing's stalks rose into the air, the black, spiked tips pointing down at him, razor sharp. Then they were lashing out, coming for him, meaning to impale him. The Dreary-thing's angry red eye was wide, alight with hunger. Dreary's own eyes fluttered wide again, focusing for just a moment as his mouth opened and groaned in torment.

DUST

The spiked stalks stopped in mid-air, a foot from James's outstretched hand. He was smiling slightly now, his own eyes alight with power and purpose.

"Wrong again, Dreary, or whoever the fuck you are," James said and spat at the thing. "I'm not a god-hunter. I'm a god-*killer!*"

The red eye's malice turned to alarm as it grew into a circular orb of surprise. James flicked his wrist up and the abomination flew into the air, crashing through the roof of the sanctuary, shards of wood and splintered rafters showering down with the rain as it came through. James curled his fingers into a fist and he waved his arm in an arc over his head. The roof above shredded into kindling and soared off into the rainy day. Droplets of water deluged the interior of the building as gray light filled the place with its pale glow. Above, something wailed and screamed.

"I didn't come to hunt N'yea'thuul down!" James howled into the stormy sky. "I came to destroy him!"

He brought his fist down to the floor as he dropped to a knee, and the Dreary-thing came down hard from the sky, smashing into the floor with a thunderous *thud*, its ten stalky tentacles scrambling in all directions and clicking across the floor as it gasped. The red eye's appearance had evolved from one of alarm to something bordering on terror. The angry mouth on its chest gnashed and bit at the air, growling and snarling and bubbling.

Behind James, he could hear the gasps of Denarius's wife and son, and the weaker, but still determined voice of his new friend speaking to him over the pelting patter of rain and the panicked sounds of the abomination that had been Gear Dreary.

"You got magic in you, suh," his friend gasped. "And there's goodness in you yet! God ain't forgotten you, Mr. James! You send it back to Hell, you hear me? Send it back to Hell!"

James spared a glance back at his friend and met the man's eyes. They were tired and drooping, but there was a fire still left in them. His stomach was torn open and blood pooled in a lake around him, though the rain was dissipating it rapidly. Marlena and Martin huddled against him, and his weak arms were curled about both their necks. He noticed the hand Marlena held over her stomach and his eyes met hers for a moment. He knew then there were more Kings yet to come, and this family could not be allowed to die. Not here. Not like this.

Not on his watch.

"To Hell, then," James said as he turned back to the Dreary-thing.

As he came around, a sharp stalk struck him across the chest, and he was soaring over Denarius and Marlena and Martin, their heads ducking and their mouths open in screams. Then he was splashing in the mud in front of the church, the wind whooshing out of him. He kicked and struggled to get to his feet, gasping for breath. Marlena and Martin were trying to pull Denarius to them, away from the doorway. Half of the front wall of the church collapsed then, smacking into the muck all around it with a thunderous crash.

The Dreary-thing was snarling and skittering forward. White-hot pain was demanding James's attention on his chest, but he ignored it, keeping his eyes focused through the rain on the monster stalking slowly toward him. Its red eye was an evil thing, shooting hate from its center like a projectile. Its bone-toothed mouth clacked open and shut. Dreary's mouth moaned as his eyes fluttered back into horrible, agonized focus.

James threw his overcoat back, exposing the revolver in the holster on his right hip.

"Come on, then!" he roared at the Dreary-thing. "Let's finish it!"

The abomination stopped then, at the edge of the structure, leering at him. Its eye blinked away the rain, but never wavered from James. Its focus was locked upon him, held in place with hunger and malevolence. The mouth on Dreary's chest almost seemed to smile then, a strange shape for the angry wound, but unmistakable nonetheless.

"The god-hunter wants a showdown," the thing snickered in a wet laugh. *"Then you shall have it!"*

Something glinted in the gray light, flashing only a moment before returning to obscurity, but it was enough for James to see. The small revolver in Dreary's hand, still gripped beneath white-knuckles and dripping with blood. Dreary moaned again from his own mouth, the eyes blinking, horribly awash in anguish.

"Your move, god-hunter," the thing spoke from the cavity in Dreary's chest, oozing bloody ichor.

James's fingers fluttered in the air above the grip of his revolver. His eyes narrowed, focused on his nemesis. The rain droned on, splashing mud and water in miniature explosions all about the muddy yard of the church. The spire collapsed above the thing then, the coiling spiral crashing through the remaining front wall and into the street to the side of the church.

Neither James nor the Dreary-thing flinched.

The mouth on the thing's chest seemed to smile again, the eye seeming to burn with anticipation. James took a deep breath, blowing it out through droplets of rain running down his face. Another glint of dim light reflected on the Bull Dog in Dreary's clutch.

Dreary's eyes fluttered open again, and James met them with his own. The cube within the dilapidated structure continued to glow with a faint blue light behind the monster, casting the figure into something just shy of a silhouette. But the eyes of his nemesis were focused now, and not only the red one on his forehead. They were wide, pained, and James noticed they had a pleading quality.

James saw something in those eyes, and he felt something within him that bordered on pity. Dreary was still alive in there, in a torment James could only imagine, and poorly at that. The anguish there was a palpable thing, and James thought of an old saying from his own time.

The enemy of my enemy is my friend.

The corner of James's mouth twitched up in a half smile and he nodded.

"Farewell, my dear Mr. James," Dreary spoke in a gurgle from his own, oozing mouth.

The red eye had just a second to twitch in confusion before Dreary raised the Bull Dog in a lightning fast motion, jabbing the barrel into the wet, red eye. There was a pop as the revolver went off and the Dreary-thing's head snapped back, the red eye bursting in a shower of crimson gel. The mouth in its chest opened wide then, a blood-chilling shriek erupting from within it. The organs writhed and slurped, but still the thing screamed, a horrifying din that almost drowned out the sound of the pummeling rain.

Another gunshot rang out, this one much sharper and louder, and the left side of Dreary's face exploded a second after James saw the man's eyes softening in the bliss and peace of death. Then brain and gristle were flying through the air as the stalks stamped wildly around in a half-circle.

James saw the smoking barrel of his Magnum in Denarius's hand as his friend's arm shook and dropped the weapon, his head falling back into his wife's bosom.

The revolver beneath James's fingers lifted from the holster and slapped into his hand. He was running then, the gun up before him, his weak hand fanning the hammer back again and again as the revolver boomed over repeatedly, the bullets finding their targets and splashing blood and meat into the soaking air. The body of the Dreary-thing jerked and spasmed with each new blast of the weapon. James winced in pain as his hurt shoulder howled in protest of its use. But he ignored it, rushing and firing away until he reached the third dry click on empty chambers.

The gun flipped twice over his finger before reseating in his holster, then James was raising both hands before him as the Dreary-thing's mouth coughed gallons of blood, wheezing and shrieking in terror, coming around to face him once more. James fell to his knees in the mud, his fingers curling into fists as he twisted his hands before him.

He screamed and wrenched his hands violently to either side.

The Dreary-thing's screams silenced then, replaced by a spine-freezing ripping of flesh and sinew as it came apart in pieces, the organs and intestines of the thing's host spilling to the mud below in a steaming heap, a mighty river of blood roiling in angry currents all around it.

Then its parts splatted to the mud, twitched for several moments, and went still.

For a full minute, perhaps longer, James remained on his knees, his fists outstretched to either side of him, breathing hard. His shoulder was pulsing with pain and he could feel the warmth of blood as it snaked down his side. His body trembled, and his gasps hitched loudly. Denarius and his family lay just inside the church, their faces running with rain, their eyes wide and astonished.

Finally, James lowered his hands.

It took him another minute to get to his feet and stumble toward the building. One side of the structure, which had to now still stood precariously, collapsed away to the ground with a loud crash. But no one seemed to take notice of this. James's eyes were zeroed in on the glowing cube, which now seemed to have grown. As he stepped onto the planks of the remains of the temple, he realized the cube hadn't grown in stature, but instead was now floating. He glanced up to the dark sky above and saw a swirling formation of clouds and streaks of lightning. He might have thought it was the onset of a tornado had he not known better. And even if he had not known better, the flittering whips of tentacles reaching out from the center of the swirling, black clouds, from the inky abyss at its center, told him the whole story.

N'yea'thuul.

"End it, Mr. James!" Marlena screamed behind him. There was real terror in her voice. James turned to her, blinking away rain, and saw her there, a hand still covering her belly in a protective manner.

He smiled at her, and nodded, rain sluicing over the brim of his hat. Then he turned back to the glowing cube beneath the swirling sky and the nightmare appendages reaching from beyond it.

"To Hell, then."

His hands came up, reaching toward the glowing cube.

37

A DREADFUL TONE erupted from the sky over them, a sort of shriek or roar, but a sound unlike anything James could associate it with. It seemed almost mechanical in a sense, a deep, droning horn, but beneath it were octaves of growling, snarling, clicking horror that were wholly sentient. His arms trembled and quivered with gooseflesh as he felt his power struggle with that of the floating, glowing marker and the god it was drawing forth from the cosmos.

James looked to the sky, raising his right hand toward it while keeping his left outstretched toward the marker. The power pushing back against his own was strong, focused. It reminded him of the first being he'd used his power against, so many years ago now. He hadn't been strong enough on his own to hold the beast off, not then. Even now, with years and years of honing his skill, of focusing his power with expert preciseness, it was a great struggle.

"It's still coming!" someone screamed behind him. He thought it was the woman, but he couldn't be sure. He couldn't devote enough attention to the words to be sure as the power of N'yea'thuul pressed back against him, breaking into the world to unleash its utter and total destruction.

The marker itself seemed to be pushing back as well. Its bluish glow was intensifying and focusing in on a central point along its face. The pressure pushing back against James intensified as a beam of blue light started protruding from its surface like a spear, coming straight at him.

No, James thought as he fell to his knees beneath the pressure from before and above him, his trembling evolving to shivers now. *Not this world. Not on my watch.*

Something warm began tickling his upper lip and the skin beneath his ears. He knew he was bleeding from the strain, so much stronger than anything he'd faced before in his life. He became aware that he'd begun screaming at some point. He wasn't sure when, but from the strain in his throat he thought it must have been for some time now. He didn't fight it. It was a release. A resolve. A way to focus his energy, his *will*, against this god of death.

The swirling clouds above began to shimmer, and the droning cry of the beast grew in volume and depth. The marker began to shimmer as well, as the blue spear inched closer and closer to James, now less than a foot from the palm of his outstretched hand. Tendrils of blue light began to stretch out from the tip of the spear of light, reaching toward him like probing fingers. A voice filled his head, though he knew it was audible only to himself. The droning shriek continued to rise and encompass everything. He was screaming louder now and could sense more than actually hear the screams of Denarius and his family behind him as they witnessed the spectacle.

Elder N'yea'thuul awaked is HERE! the voice in his mind roared at him in an alien tongue he nonetheless understood. *Accept this fate. Accept N'yea'thuul!*

His vision tinted red all at once and he began blinking away a coppery warmth as the rain cleared his vision. He was nearing the end of his rope, the end of his strength. He was very weak now, wanting nothing more than to relinquish his power and collapse beneath the weight of the Elder and its will.

A vision conjured in his mind then, part of a memory from many years before. It was a graveyard from his own time and place. Three people he loved more than anyone in all the world, walking away, their backs to him. A fourth person, a baby in the arms of the woman, his little eyes blinking with awe as they focused on him. Eyes that bore a striking resemblance to his own, though he wasn't sure why he thought so. It had been merely an instant, nothing more. They hadn't known he was there, his family and the one he'd left to watch over them, and that was for the best. He'd still had worlds to travel and gods to kill. But he'd peeked in on them, saw them happy, and that had been enough.

Then he saw the woman and the man, his best friends, with his daughter Joanna and the baby boy the woman had been holding, screaming in the midst of destruction as fire fell from the sky, melting their skin and turning their cries to smoky gasps.

James bared his teeth.

The blue tendrils from the spear of light inched closer still, the voice of N'yea'thuul taunting him in his mind, and his scream rose in decibel and pitch as he focused every ounce of his gift at the sky and the marker and what they brought with them.

"NOOOOOO!" he cried in a thunderous, booming voice.

There was a burst of energy then, the shimmering sky and the shimmering marker suddenly awash in wavering light. The drone of the god in the sky sharpened then, a sound of something like alarm, and then a *shuh-whump* of sound, as of all sound and air being sucked into a vacuum all at once, whipped out from him in a cloud of shimmering energy.

The abyss at the center of the swirling sky imploded in on itself, and gone were the flailing tentacles and the cry of the elder god. The clouds ceased their swirling and the rain filled its absence.

At the same moment, the blue spear of light, with its tendrils of fingers, folded in on itself and vanished back into the marker. It shone brilliantly for a full two seconds before emitting its own *shuh-whump* of energy and splitting down the center, falling to the floor of the sanctuary. The two pieces wobbled unsurely for a moment before one side toppled over and crushed the stairs beneath it. The other side came to stillness, and all sound but the pelting drops of rain vanished into the sky.

James held his position for a moment longer before allowing his arms to fall to his sides as he emptied his lungs with a loud, exasperated sigh of air. He heaved breaths for several seconds before turning his head around to Denarius, Marlena, and Martin.

Their faces were all identical masks of awe as they stared back at him with something like amazement and fear in equal measures. James tried to smile, but only managed a grimace. He hoped they took his meaning.

Then his world went black as he sprawled onto the floor.

38

FAINT VOICES DRIFTED to his ears, coming in and out of the focus of his hearing. Something brushed across his face. He could feel the now cooling blood wiped away from his face, replaced by a light drizzle of cool moisture. He tried opening his eyes, but all he could see was a haze of shapes in the gloom, then his eyes were shut again.

"... *otta wake up, Mr. Ja* ... " a voice drifted to him momentarily before washing back out in a garbled tide. "... *an't die on u* ... "

He tried blinking again, this time with slightly better results. The thing wiped over his face again, and when he fluttered open his eyes, he could just make out the face of Marlena, her eyes concerned and her mouth frowning. Her hair was matted and wild, caked blood on the side of her scalp where she'd been grazed by Dreary's bullet, but James thought she was a sight to behold in that moment, beautiful and transcendent. He tried to smile.

"You just wake up now, y'hear?" Marlena said. "My husband needs your help!"

That brought him out of his fog. James rolled to his side, slowly, wincing from the ache in his shoulder, his body protesting all over. He was tired. Drained. Hurt badly. But Denarius was worse. Though he didn't know what she expected he could do for the man, he decided to get off the floor anyway.

She moved aside as he made it over onto his knees. He stayed like that for several seconds, catching his breath and curling his hurt arm up to his chest. Then he peered up from beneath the brim of his hat at Denarius and his heart sank.

Denarius was on his back, his head resting in his son's lap, hand clasped tightly in Martin's. He was shaking all over, gasping for breath, his eyes blinking wildly. The rain had eased to a light drizzle in the time James had been unconscious, though he had no idea how long that had been. Could have been a few seconds or half an hour. He didn't know, and it didn't matter. And when his eyes fell to the red horror on Denarius's stomach, he knew nothing he might do now would matter either.

"Oh, Christ," James muttered, barely audible.

He crawled toward his new friend shakily, taking in the wound in his belly as he did. It was gashed open badly, and a tangled loop of what looked like lower intestine hung out of the ragged flesh.

Martin was crying, soaked through to the bone, his teeth bared in mourning.

"Daddy," the boy wept, rocking on his rump. "Daddy, you can't die, no suh, daddy! This man gonna fix you right up!"

Denarius's eyes moved slowly and met his son's. He didn't say anything, only smiled warmly at his boy, a knowing look on his face. Martin seemed to glean his meaning at once as his sobs intensified and he buried his face next to that of his father's. Marlena scooted over next to Denarius, looked at his wound with a grimace for a moment, then looked to James.

"I seen you use that magic, suh," she said in a wavering voice. "You can fix my man's belly! You can fix—"

James was shaking his head before Denarius cut her off, a look of helpless anguish coming over his face.

"Marlena, darlin'," Denarius managed through a cough of blood. "Baby, it ain't that kind of ma . . . magic."

He rolled to his side enough to cough out a pint of slimy blood onto the wet planks. He spat twice before rolling his head back into his son's lap and meeting their eyes in turn.

"Mr. James Dee got magic in him, alright," Denarius said and managed a pained smile. "But it ain't the healin' kind, I'm afraid."

Martin and Marlena's eyes both flooded with tears then as they stared down at Denarius for a moment before turning on James in unison, their expressions desperate and full of crumbling hope.

James only shook his head once and lowered his gaze to Denarius.

"I wish to Christ I could do something, Denarius," James said, reaching out and taking the man's hand in his own. "I wish like hell I could."

Denarius nodded through his shudders, which were now intensifying, and managed another smile, more diminished this time.

"I know that, Mr. Dee," he said. "And I told you, you got good in you yet. You done saved this here world, suh. Ain't no bad man would save the world. Ain't no bad man would save my family. You remember that, ya hear? Ain't no bad man would do that."

Denarius squeezed James's hand then and nodded. James squeezed back.

"It's been an honor knowing you, Denarius."

Denarius smiled wearily. "An honor knowing you, Mr. Dee."

James laughed then and shook his head. Marlena turned to him, her eyes narrowing.

"What you find funny, now of all times, mister?" she asked, a hint of venom creeping into her voice.

James held his other hand out to her in a calming gesture.

"I'm sorry, ma'am," he started and tried his hardest to covey his empathy to her through his eyes. "It's just, *Dee* ain't really my name so much as it's an initial."

Denarius and Marlena both looked at him with perplexed qualities. Martin paid none of them any mind as he wept on his father's shoulder.

"When I came here from my own time and place," James said as he shrugged, "well, I had to leave everything I knew and loved behind. At some point along the way, I lost sight of who I was deep down. The calling, the *mission*, what have you, it became everything. I started using my Christian name with just the initial of my last. Not really sure why, but I did."

Denarius raised his head ever so slightly. It looked like a monumental effort to James.

"Then what's your name, suh? Your *real* name, I mean?"

James smiled widely at his friend, tears stinging his own eyes now.

"My friends call me Jim," he said. "Jim Dalton."

They all stayed like that for several seconds. Finally, Denarius started to nod and lay his head back. He went into another coughing fit, the sound of phlegm and blood bubbling past his lips throughout. When he was still, he smiled at James through blood-soaked teeth.

"Jim Dalton," he said, trying the words out. "I like that. A hell of a lot better name than *James Dee.*"

James—*Jim*—couldn't help but laugh at this. Though Denarius was unable to laugh with him, he smiled, as did Marlena, though her smile was markedly sadder than her husband's.

James finished his laugh, squeezed his friend's hand once more, and released him. They all seemed to understand he was giving them their privacy with Denarius, and Marlena and Martin focused back on him.

"Boy," Denarius said in a tremulous voice, as though speaking were a great effort, "you take care of your mama now, ya hear?"

Martin's eyes flooded with tears as he nodded in the affirmative to his father, sobs breaking through as he tried to hold them in.

"You the man now. And you gonna have to help her get ready for your baby brother or sister."

Martin's eyes went wide with shock then, as did Marlena's.

"You knew?" she asked Denarius.

He turned to her, holding her hand close to his chest, and nodded.

"I seen how you was protecting that tummy of yours," he said and chuckled. "Same as you did when Martin was in there and we be out working them fields."

Several agonized laughs escaped him, though he seemed to be enjoying the moment rather than resenting it.

"You always was careful 'bout not lettin' *nothin'* harm that baby. And you'll have Martin to help you now."

He smiled at her again as her face contorted in a rictus of grief and what might have been joy at once. She sobbed loudly and covered her mouth a moment later.

"Don't you cry now," Denarius said, trying to calm her. "Ain't no good for the baby. Got him to think about, now."

She took a few breaths, nodding rapidly, then pulled her hand away to reveal an anguished smile of her own.

"So, you think it's a boy, do ya?"

Denarius nodded. "I sho-nuff do, Missus King. I always move my hips just right to make boys when we have time to ourselves."

She wept with laughter then, giving him a light, playful shove on the shoulder. Denarius was grinning widely back at his wife in spite of his visible pain. Martin still seemed to be in shock.

"D-daddy?" the boy asked when the laughter subsided.

Denarius turned to him. "Yes, son?"

"I'm gonna make you proud, daddy," he said, his face serious. "Imma take good care of mama and the baby. You'll see. I'll make you proud. You'll see from . . . from . . . "

He broke down into fresh sobs then as Denarius reached up and stroked his son's face with the tips of his fingers, calming the child.

"Martin," Denarius said with admiration in his tone. "You been making me proud since the day you's born, boy. Ain't nothing you could *ever* do would change how proud I am to have you as my son."

James turned away from them then, nursing his wounded shoulder and walked back toward the ruined marker. He felt he was intruding on their final moments and meant to give them the privacy they deserved. As he made his way, he glanced out past the collapsed wall and saw several people standing outside, their eyes wide and jaws slack. His first reaction was to go for his gun, but a second glance told him there was no need. These people weren't here to cause them harm. Those who had meant harm had died in the battle outside and within the church. These were merely those who'd been trapped here against their will, now in stupefied awe of their newfound freedom.

He turned from them and looked upon the broken marker. Its markings were dark, and no glow emitted from its inky depths now. It was little more than a ruined artifact.

He held out his good arm, waved it beneath where the pieces of the marker lay, and both heard and felt the rumble as rock and earth moved at his will. Moments later, the rumbling reached a crescendo and the floor and the ground beneath swallowed the pieces of the obsidian cube. It vanished beneath the dirt and rubble, out of sight.

He waited there like that, staring down at the spot where the marker had vanished, for a long time. When he finally turned back toward the King family, he saw Denarius was no longer moving, his eyes closed and his chest still. Martin wept on his shoulder, still holding his father's limp hand, as Marlena rose to her feet, wiping tears from her face.

James didn't move as she made her way to him slowly down the aisle, only stopping when she was two feet in front of him.

"Mr. Ja—um—Jim," she said, her eyes on a spot on the floor between them.

"Yes, ma'am," he replied.

She met his eyes. "I'm sure you'd like some rest. Lord knows my boy and I could use some. But my husband needs a . . . a proper burial. I wondered if you might help me see to it."

He smiled at the anguished woman as warmly as he could.

"It would be my honor, Missus King."

They made their way back to Denarius and the weeping Martin then, joining hands as they made their way, taking strength from each other. Outside, the onlookers began to wander about, confused and unsure. But things would be set to rights soon enough, James knew. And this damned town would have a chance to be reborn.

As he reached his fallen friend, the sun began breaking through the clouds above.

EPILOGUE

DENARIUS WAS BURIED up by the ridge where he and James had come into town early that morning. With the sun shining over the town, the shimmering waters of the lake danced with prisms of light and birds began to sing as the world seemed to come back to life. Some of the townsfolk had helped, though James had done most of the work with a twirl of his hands.

Prayers were said and, at the end, James had made the sign of the cross over his chest, something he hadn't done in a very long time. It felt good to do it, and even he prayed for his fallen friend. He had stayed with Marlena and Martin for a time as the townsfolk wandered back to wherever they had come from, out of habit or with some purpose of destination, he didn't know. The temperature had risen when the sun came out, and beads of sweat now cropped on his brow. He wiped them away with the back of his hand.

"Gettin' warm out," Marlena said, glancing up into the trail leading into the woods.

James nodded. "Where will you and the boy go?"

She glanced at him, then back down to the fresh grave where her husband lay, and shrugged.

"Oh, I don't know," she said. "Ain't much back at our house, and Martin and I can't keep up the fields without . . . with . . . "

She took a breath, covering her mouth with her knuckles a moment, and exhaled slowly. Then she went on.

"I don't much care for the idea of being far from Denarius," she said.

James nodded, looking down at Marin. He ruffled his hair, though Martin didn't seem to notice. Then he looked back to Marlena.

"There's plenty of things to be done here, you know?"

She looked at him, confused for a moment, blinking rapidly.

"Stay here, you mean, suh?" she asked.

He nodded. "Just a thought. This place could really be something nice if the right person were to see to the town. There's still plenty of townsfolk around who'd likely be eager to build something decent out of what's been here all these years." He shrugged. "Just a thought."

She seemed to consider this, looked to Martin and then to the grave, then to her belly before returning her eyes to his.

"Where will you go?" she asked.

James looked up to the sky. Most of the clouds were gone now, and he squinted against the bright light of the day.

"I been traveling for far too many years," he said. "But I can't stay here. I don't belong. Denarius taught me that, I reckon. Though I don't think he ever realized it. A man's place is with his family. A *good* man's place, that is. And I've been gone from mine far too long."

She nodded and placed a hand on his wounded shoulder. He winced, and she pulled away, apologizing.

"We need to see to that before you go," she said.

He waved her off. "Where I'm going, they've got a lot better ways of caring for a wound like this. I wouldn't argue with you if you were to offer to clean it up and put it in a sling, however."

She smiled and nodded.

"Of course, Mr. Dalton."

They made their way back to town and Marlena cleaned his wound and made a sling for his arm out of some cloth she found in the old General Store. Then she and James left Martin on the porch of the store and walked the short distance to the now destroyed temple of the Elder. As they passed the stained floor and the still lying bodies of several men, he stopped, eyeing something on the floor. He stooped and snatched it up, turned it over in his hand a few times, then held it out to Marlena.

"What's this?" she asked, taking the battered book in her hands.

"That's Mr. Gear Dreary's book of the Elders," he said, nodding to the tome. "Destroy it, keep it, whatever. Just don't let anyone else get it."

She looked at him, her dark eyes narrowed.

"What's out there, Mr. Dalton?" she asked, nodding to the sky. "Out there. Wherever that thing come from?"

James looked to the sky a moment, then down at the floor.

"It's all in that book, if you feel the need to know about it. But I'll tell ya, I think you'd be happier not knowing."

She didn't say anything, and several moments later he nodded at her, tipping his hat, and began to move toward the center of the aisle. He raised his hand, made a waving motion, and the air before him began to shimmer, a small warble coming to their ears. The sound began to rise slowly, and as it did, he turned back to Marlena one last time, a curious look on his face.

"What will you name him?" he asked.

Marlena looked confused for a moment, hugging the book to her stomach. Then she looked down, pulling the book away and letting her hands fall to her hips. She met his eyes again, the hint of a smile at the corner of her mouth.

"You think it's a boy too, do ya?" she asked with a small laugh.

"Ma'am," he said, shrugging, "if Denarius says it's a boy, I'm inclined to agree with the man."

They shared a short but genuine laugh.

"Stephen," Marlena said finally as the last chuckles faded.

James nodded, pursing his lips, and almost laughed. He held it in, though, and smiled at her.

"Stephen King, huh?" he said, and this time couldn't contain a small bark of laughter.

"Something funny about that," she asked, putting a hand to one hip.

James shook his head and held his hand up in surrender.

"No, ma'am," he said, and laughed again. "Least not for another hundred years or so."

Marlena's head cocked to the side in confusion. James just waved and turned back to the shimmering air before him. He had places to go and a family to find. He could finally feel the comfort in his heart of a man at peace with himself, something he had not felt in a long time.

You have a pure heart, but you're not a good man.

He smiled as he began stepping through the shimmering portal, back to all he knew and loved. He'd always had a pure heart, but he was finally starting to believe he was a decent man as well, deep down beneath all the mire.

Jim Dalton vanished from sight as the shimmering faded from the air around him and made his way back to where he belonged.

ABOUT THE AUTHOR

Chris Miller is a native Texan who began telling and writing down stories at an early age. He began publishing in 2017 with his first novel, *A Murder of Saints*. Since then, he has released multiple novels as well as a novella. He has also been inducted into many anthologies where he has appeared alongside many literary titans. When not writing, he enjoys playing guitar, watching movies, and spending time with his family. He is happily married to the love of his life, Aliana, and they have three beautiful children. He lives in Winnsboro, TX.

Made in the USA
Columbia, SC
30 March 2022